ALSO BY ELIZABETH EULBERG

The Lonely Hearts Club

Prom & Prejudice

Take a Bow

Revenge of the Girl with the Great Personality

Better Off Friends

We Can Work It Out

ELIZABETH EULBERG

Point

Library of Congress Cataloging-in-Publication Data

Names: Eulberg, Elizabeth, author.
Title: Just another girl / Elizabeth Eulberg.
Desription: New York, NY: Scholastic Press, [2017] | Summary:
Sixteen-year-old Hope has known Brady most of her life, and they are close friends and members of the Rube Goldberg Club at high school, but Hope has always believed they would be more than friends, so when Parker becomes his girlfriend, Hope views the newcomer as a rival--but Parker has secrets, and when circumstances force the two girls together Hope realizes that Parker is really just another girl.
Identifiers: LCCN 2016037799 | ISBN 9780545956284 (hardcover)
Subjects: LCSH: Interpersonal relations–Juvenile fiction. | Dating (Social customs)–Juvenile fiction. | Friendship–Juvenile fiction. | High schools–Juvenile fiction. | Science clubs–Juvenile fiction. | Secrecy–Juvenile fiction. | CYAC: Interpersonal relations–Fiction. | Dating (Social customs)–Fiction. | Friendship–Fiction. | High schools–Fiction. | Schools–Fiction. | Science clubs–Fiction. | Secrets–Fiction.
Classification: LCC PZ7.E8685 Ju 2017 | DDC 813.6 [Fic] –dc23 LC record available at https://lccn.loc.gov/2016037799

ISBN 978-0-545-95628-4

10 9 8 7 6 5 4 3 2 1   17 18 19 20 21

Printed in the U.S.A.   23
First edition, April 2017

Book design by Abby Dening

For Jackson Pearce, who planted the
seed for this book years ago,
and Jen Calonita, who has had to listen
to me talk about it ever since.

Hope

40 DAYS AWAY

This is it, I tell myself.

"Are you ready?" Brady asks as he leans into me. "Although when aren't you prepared for total world domination?"

"Precisely. It's about time you noticed," I reply with a flip of my hair. Brady always brings out my sassy side, and my flirty side, and my I-love-you-so-much-it-hurts-sometimes side.

Brady knows every side of me, except for that last one. How can a person be so close to somebody, literally and figuratively, yet be so painfully blind?

Maybe things will be different now. Maybe this is when everything will change.

He winks at me behind his black rectangular frames, his dark, messy hair partly obscuring his vision.

I'm always telling myself, *Maybe now. Maybe this.*

I'm always telling myself, *This is it.*

"Oh, I've been noticing that about you since, hmm, the beginning of time," Brady says. "Or at least first grade, which for all intents and purposes is the beginning of time. It was unmistakable."

"Greatness is like that," I fire back.

Brady and I face each other, him with his arms folded, me with eyes narrowed. It's a standoff to see who is going to relinquish their banter throne first. It's always like this with us, one-upping each other in ridiculousness until someone breaks.

I bite the insides of my cheeks to keep from smiling.

"Ah, guys? Can we do this?" Dan calls out from the machine. He exchanges a look with Conor. They always get annoyed when Brady and I spend the majority of our time together being . . . well, being *us*.

But, hey, it's my club and I'll flirt if I want to.

Why? a dark part of me wonders. *Why do you keep torturing yourself? Why are* you *so blind that* you *can't see that he's just—*

No.

"Saved, once again, by the siren call of Rube Goldberg," I whisper to Brady before I turn my attention to the machine that's been taunting and teasing us for weeks now. "Okay, let's do this."

Brady gives me his biggest smile, the one that melts every inch of me.

He puts his hand on my arm.

I don't think he even knows what he's doing.

Or maybe he knows exactly what he's doing.

I never know for sure.

The project. Focus on the project, I tell myself, trying to chase out the butterflies in my stomach so another species of butterfly—the kind that cares about school projects and grades and the future blah, blah, blah—can move in. There's no more avoiding the truth. This is when I find out if our countless hours and months of work have paid off.

No pressure or anything.

But here's the thing: I'm not really nervous. Okay, I'm a little worried it won't work, but I look over at Brady and know that with him by my side, I can do anything.

That's the way it's always been between us, so I have no doubt we'll succeed. Eventually.

"Do you want to do the honors?" Dan asks as he gently places a small blue-and-white marble in my hand.

We hold our collective breath as I walk up to the machine we spent the better part of last semester working on. I wish I could say I have no idea how I got involved in this, but the answer is one word, and it starts with a *B*. It's a very simple story: Brady was obsessed with Rube Goldberg machines. I was obsessed with Brady. So *voilà*! I started the club so we could work on the machines together. Emphasis, in my mind, on the word *together*.

And the weird thing is, I think that's why he went for it, too. So we could have something together. But neither of us was brave enough to admit that. We never are. *Especially* me. It's like our relationship is one of these crazy contraptions we build—one false move and the whole thing falls apart. So you spend all your time making sure you don't knock things off course. Even if you think that maybe there might be an even better course you could be on, if only there weren't . . . obstacles.

I position the marble at the start of our contraption and say a silent prayer as I let go. The marble makes its way down a ramp. It then knocks over the first in a series of dominos in an S-shaped formation. All eight eyes in the room intently watch as each domino goes tumbling down, creating the perfect chain reaction. The last domino sets off a mousetrap, which snaps so loudly, I jump a bit. Then the string attached to the mousetrap pulls down on a lever and . . . nothing.

The machine stops. The balloon hanging at the end remains limp.

"What happened?" Conor grumbles as we examine the other side of the pulley, where a spoon's supposed to snap up, releasing a ball.

"We don't have enough momentum." Brady leans down to look at the string, his hands behind his back to reduce the risk of knocking anything over.

"Back to the drawing board, I guess," I reply, hiding any disappointment in my voice.

If I've learned anything in my sixteen years on this planet, it's that anything worth having takes work. Anything can be accomplished with the three Ps: Patience, Planning, and Perseverance.

That voice of hope pops back into my head. *Maybe now. Maybe this.*

"Don't give up," Brady says.

It's hard not to take that as some sort of sign.

I'm always looking for signs.

Spotting them is easy. Reading them, though—that's the part I always seem to get wrong. It's frustrating how easily you can misinterpret something when you only want to believe in one thing.

I pull on the string. "It's still not as tight as we need it to be." I grab some glue and lift the mousetrap up. "This needs to be firmly planted down in order for the snap to work properly."

Dan comes over to help me press down on the trap while Brady and Conor watch. "I think you're right. Once this is properly secured, this will be a *snap!* Get it? *SNAP?*"

We all groan. Not only is Dan unaware that his attempts at humor are outright embarrassing, he genuinely thinks he's a comedian. We put up with it because Dan's the smartest science and math student we've got.

"We'll get this," Conor reassures us. He then puts his hands on his hips and sticks his chest out. (I think he's trying to emulate a superhero. I don't want to tell him he looks less like Superman and more like he's constipated.) "Even darkness must pass. A new day will come. And when the sun shines, it will shine out clearer."

At least with Dan, I have some idea what he's talking about. Conor relies upon quoting from Tolkien or making Dungeons & Dragons references.

As for Brady?

Well, I'm fluent in Brady-isms. I know he'd say the same about me.

Brady leans in to inspect my work on the mousetrap and places his hand on the small of my back. "Looks like you've saved the day, Hope."

There's another sign. Someone who's "just" a friend would move his hand away from my back as soon as the sentence was done.

Yet his hand remains.

"Yes! Once again, Hope gives us hope," Dan says with a snort before adjusting his wire-rimmed glasses.

We all groan even louder this time as Conor hits Dan with the notebook we're using to map out our machine.

Brady's hand remains on my back.

Mr. Sutton, our science teacher and club advisor, walks into his classroom, asking for an update. Dan and Conor begin giving an overly descriptive account of our failed run-through. They try to make it sound positive, but Mr. Sutton doesn't look pleased. Which starts to stress me out.

Brady and I decide to hang back. He finally removes his hand, but I can still feel the heat of its imprint. He lets out a small sigh, which signals to me that he's stressed, too.

This has to work. It *has* to.

I look up at him, wondering what we can do. In response, he wraps his arms around me.

"Don't worry," he says, his voice so reassuring. "We have plenty of time to make it work."

He's talking about us.

No, he's not.

But he could be.

No, I remind myself. *He's talking about the project. Don't be so delusional.*

We're six weeks away from a Rube Goldberg contest in Cleveland, and if we win, our team will go to the national competition in Indiana. A lot can happen in six weeks.

He gives me another squeeze before letting go and bumping me with his hip. "Plus, I'd never underestimate the girl who once single-handedly bowled a whopping twenty-two."

"How dare you insult my athletic prowess!" I give him a look of horrified shock, complete with an exaggeratedly open mouth and my hand on my heart. "Plus, you know, I was *nine*."

"You were using bumpers! Is that even mathematically possible?" He gets out a notebook and pretends to do a few calculations.

"Give me that." I try to grab the notebook, but Brady holds it over his head. Since he's six four, he might as well put it on Mars. There's no way I can reach it. Unless . . .

See, I know Brady better than anyone. I know everything about him, especially his weaknesses. I glance down at a bare stretch of his stomach that's currently exposed.

I look up at him with a smirk.

His eyes get wide. "What? What are you going to do?"

That's when I attack. I start tickling the spot above his right armpit, where he's the most sensitive. He crouches down and tries to wiggle away, but now I have him pinned against the desk.

"Mercy!" he screams between laughs.

"You know that's not what I want to hear."

"Fine! Fine!" He holds his hands up in surrender. "Spit-rat! Spit-rat!"

(Mr. Sutton, Dan, and Conor all give us looks. They're not fluent in our secret language. I always wished Brady and I could merge our names together like people do with celebrity couples, but Hody never caught on, as much as I tried.)

I give Brady a satisfied smile as I take his notebook from him. As I suspected, he wasn't doing math. Instead he wrote, *Dear Diary, is it possible for Hope to be the worst bowler of all time?*

"Very funny, ha ha." I fake pout.

"A little help here," Dan says, not hiding his annoyance.

"Admit it, you love it when I mock," Brady whispers to me as we approach the machine.

"I'll admit to no such thing, Mr. Lambert," I reply coldly, doing my best to suppress the smile I always have in his company.

"Come on." He wiggles his eyebrows at me; his left one sports a scar I have studied for what feels like most of my life.

I was there when Brady got that scar, the summer after third grade. We were running to the ice-cream truck when Brady, always the opposite of graceful, tripped over his own feet and a tree trunk interrupted his fall. I ran the two blocks to his house to get his mom and held his hand while he got stitches.

Every time I skim through the meticulous scrapbooks my memory makes, he's there.

Our elementary school Christmas concert with matching reindeer antlers and red noses as we sang "Rudolph, the Red-Nosed Reindeer" as if our Christmas presents depended upon it . . .

Him in our swimming pool for my eighth-grade graduation party, and me realizing how his body had changed . . .

Our first kiss, when I was nine and he was ten . . . we'd been playing hide-and-seek, hiding from his older brother, Zach. We were crouched down behind a bush, trying not to laugh and shake the branches to give away our location. "Stop it!" I scolded him as he kept pulling on my ponytail. He laughed, kissed me on the lips, and then ran away . . .

No one's running anymore. Whenever we're in the same room, we're drawn together like magnets.

It's not all in my head. He also feels it.

I know it. He knows it.

Yet we pretend we don't, since it's easier. Or at least we pretend it's easier, even if it feels harder. But the *maybe now* is always there. It's always taunting me.

Maybe this time, my mind begins to repeat in an unrelenting loop.

Brady looks at the broken machine. "We totally got this. We've got the biggest brain in school and the coolest girl in the history of cool girls. I probably should add that Conor and I are aware we are here solely for our looks."

I sigh heavily. "If that's the case, we're in more trouble than I thought."

Brady pokes me in the side, where he knows *I'm* ticklish.

We all get back to work on the task at hand. I steal one more glance at Brady and he gives me his crooked smile that always lifts my spirits.

There's no doubt in my mind we're going to make this machine a success.

Patience. Planning. Perseverance.

I've had the Patience to know something as special as Brady and me will take time to work itself out.

I've been following a Plan to ensure that, despite being in high school (when some friendships drift apart), we've remained close.

And Perseverance. I was the one he came to when he had a crush on Cynthia Madden in eighth grade. I was the first person he called when she broke his heart by going out with Timothy Heinz. I was the one who went shopping with him when he wanted to get Sandra Cohn a Valentine's Day gift his freshman year. Me. It's always been me.

But I can only control so much. While I've followed my *P*s to the letter, there's another *P* who's managed to get in the way. A *P* who's annoyingly stayed rooted by Brady's side since freshman year. A *P* I can't seem to shake, no matter how hard I try.

A *P* who's now standing in the doorway of the classroom, saying his name.

He turns away from me. He goes to her.

His actual, real-life girlfriend.

Parker.

39 DAYS AWAY

It's hard to keep a secret in a small town.

I've been going to the same school with the same people since middle school, when the two elementary schools combined our class to the whopping seventy-eight people we are today. Everybody knows everybody. If you skip school, someone in the community will see you and call your parents. You can't flunk a class without four different people saying something to them at the one grocery store in town. If you have a crush on a guy, there's a distinct probability he'll hear about it from a friend. Or a teacher. Or a parent. Or his dentist.

That's why I've kept my real feelings for Brady close to me. Everybody in town knows we've been practically attached at the hip since we were little. But only as friends. (It always stings when someone refers to us as friends. We're much more than that. Even if I'm starting to feel as if that's all we'll ever be.)

The only person I've entrusted with my true feelings is my best friend, Madelyn. Not only do I know every one of her deep, dark secrets, but I'm positive she'd never be tempted to betray me. Madelyn's the kind of person who doesn't give a crap about what anybody thinks of her.

Unfortunately (and embarrassingly), I'm the opposite. I care immensely about what people think. I blame the small-town mentality of wanting to get along with the people I've been forced to be around every day since birth. I'm starting to get an itch to do something, be someone people can't help but notice, to make a mark. Be someone that Brady can't ignore his true feelings for.

"You do realize time is ticking?" Madelyn feels the need to remind me at lunch the next day. She drags a french fry through her tailor-made special dipping sauce, which is a sickening pink combination of catsup and mayonnaise. "I'm fully aware I'm a song on repeat on this particular matter."

Yes, she is. Brady's a senior. I'm a junior. We have less than five months until his graduation. Madelyn's of the mind-set I should come out and tell Brady how I feel. Just like she did last year before homecoming, when she went right up to James Lincoln and told him she thought he was hot and that she wanted to do something with him that night, "be it the dreaded high school ritualistic experience of a dance or something more daring."

She didn't even bat an eyelash when he laughed right in her face. She walked away with a shrug and moved on to her next crush, a guy she met online on some alternative-music website.

Even now when we pass James and his friends, he'll say some cutting remark about her. Because of her all-black clothing, short jet-black hair with a navy blue streak in it, and heavy, dark eye makeup (but always with a classic red lip), two of his go-to insults are *the walking dread* and *zombie loser*. Madelyn laughs right back at him, referring to him as "my slight mental error in judgment of one's character."

There's no way, and I mean *no way*, I could ever be so bold, no matter the situation. I'd cower if a guy ever said that to me, just like I've been cowering behind the truth with Brady. I couldn't handle it if he rejected me. Everything we have now—the banter, the touching, the promise we might someday be *more*—would be gone. I'd have to let go of all that. So as much as it pains me, I'd rather have a pretend something with him than nothing at all.

Although I guess Madelyn does have a point.

Maybe now, the voice rings in my head.

Why *not* now?

All signs are present: a lingering hand here, a blushing face after another compliment there. Just last week he told me on our walk to the parking lot after a meeting that when he thought about college, he was excited—but then he looked me straight in the eye and said, "I'm just worried about all the things I'll miss."

He made a conscious decision to stop and look at me as he said those words. How can I simply disregard that?

"Have you ever used a hamster wheel for your contraptions?" Madelyn asks.

"No," I reply, looking longingly at her fries. "While it could generate some energy or motion, it's basically something that keeps going around and around, not really going— Oh." I stop, realizing Madelyn's furthering her case for me to finally step up to the plate.

Point Madelyn.

"Remember that time a screw or whatever got in the way of your thingy?" While it's clear Madelyn can't recall specific details, it's sweet she remembers some of the constant babbling I've done about the different machines, along with the many, many problems I've had, in and outside of the club.

"Of course."

I doubt I could forget. We used a tube shaped like a corkscrew. A small ball was supposed to go down it to hit a lever at the end, but the ball kept getting stuck. It took us nearly a week to figure out that when we screwed in the tube to keep it upright, the screw went too far in and a piece of plastic had blocked the ball from passing through.

"All you need for a clear path to Brady's heart is to get rid of the blockage," Madelyn replies.

There's no need for her to clarify what the blockage is in my scenario. I keep glancing over at her as she sits with Brady. With her shiny, straight, long, blond hair and her perfect little body.

It's truly amazing that someone so tiny can be such a huge obstacle.

But it's not only the fact that Parker's pretty and petite. It's that she's THE WORST. THE ABSOLUTE WORST. I can count on one hand the number of times we've spoken. Whenever I've attempted to talk to her, it's like this ordeal I'm forcing her to endure. If I'm fortunate enough and catch her when she's feeling generous, she'll nod and acknowledge my presence. But she can never quite hide the fact that she'd rather be with anyone else.

That makes two of us.

I've heard people say opposites attract, but I don't get it. Brady's warm, while Parker's cold and distant. Brady's funny, while I don't think I've ever seen Parker crack a smile outside of her little circle.

How could he want to be with someone like that?

"Look, Hope, you know I'm willing to have the same conversation over and over again, but three years is starting to become my limit. You need to have some sort of deadline of when things need to happen," Madelyn states matter-of-factly, as if it's that simple. "If not, you're going to be forty years old, telling yourself that your time will come, only after his children graduate college and his wife dies of natural causes."

I grimace at her because she's right. It's embarrassing how pathetic I've become. How I hold on to every small interaction. How I keep making excuses for why I can't come clean to him. If I'd been up-front years ago, who knows where we'd be now.

It *has* to be now or never.

No more *maybe* now, simply *now*.

Oh God, I'm going to be sick.

No. I'm going to do something for once.

I reach into my bag to pull out the calendar I keep for the club. I've begun a daily countdown to the competition, to keep track of how much time we have left and everything we still need to accomplish. At least that was the original intention. With my index finger, I trace the date that's been circled since the start of the school year.

"The competition." It's thirty-nine days away. I have thirty-nine days to put a Plan into place to finally make Brady mine. Bit by bit, I'll Persevere to ensure that by that weekend I'll get my desired outcome. (Maybe it's time to throw Patience to the curb—haven't I demonstrated enough Patience?) "We'll be in Cleveland together. Just the two of us."

"Yes, just the two of you and Dan and Conor and Mr. Sutton," Madelyn says as she turns her attention to the slice of pepperoni pizza in front of her. "Isn't your mom threatening to come along?"

"She's staying home," I state solely to assure myself. Mom's been extremely supportive of the club. She's that mom who enthusiastically supports me in anything I do. To some people she may seem a little clingy. (Okay, the people are me, and she can be a lot clingy most of the time.) I keep reminding myself it's simply a by-product of me being an only child who was born premature after my parents had struggled for years to conceive. (Hence my name.)

"I bet you a vintage vinyl she'll find a way to come," Madelyn dares me with a smirk. "No way she's going to let her precious baby girl go off to the big bad metropolis of Cleveland without her."

It's a bet I'm not willing to take, as I know Mom will find a way to come. She always finds a way. Angrily, I stab a lettuce leaf with a plastic fork and it breaks in two.

"That's what you get for trying to eat like a rabbit." Madelyn pushes her half-eaten slice at me. "Okay, try to convince me you don't want this instead."

My stomach betrays me by growling. I'm hungry. This stupid diet I found online where I only eat food that existed back in the caveman days isn't working. I want bread. I want cheese. I want real food.

I happily pick up Madelyn's slice and take a bite, savoring the finest cheesy, greasy goodness the high school cafeteria can provide.

"Plus, we both know Brady likes a girl who can eat," Madelyn goes on, tilting her head in the direction of the table in the center of the cafeteria, where Brady and Parker sit with their friends. Parker's tray always overflows with food, despite the fact that she's a stick figure. "Although if that was all he wanted, we know he'd be madly in love with *me*."

She takes out a candy bar and starts eating it with a wistful smile on her face. She prides herself on eating whatever she wants, whenever she wants. She's been buying clothes in the "plus" section of stores since sixth grade. (According to Madelyn, "there are few places that can even attempt to contain all I've got to offer.") So far, I've still been able to shop in the Juniors section, squeezing my hips and thighs into a size ten on a good day.

The first time I brought a salad to lunch, Madelyn moved her nose so her silver-hoop nose ring wiggled in protest. "That is so boring," she commented. "We're all going to die someday. I'd rather do it with my mouth full of delicious food."

I wish I had even a tenth of her confidence.

I look over at Parker, with her skinny body, as she eats the second sandwich on her plate. She's listening to one of her friends tell a story, her usual resting bitch face on. The only time I see her smile or show any emotion is when she has Brady's undivided attention.

I don't want to be one of those girls who hates on other girls, but it's so hard with Parker. It's impossible to like her, even for Brady's sake. She's a walking reminder of everything I don't have. There are days I don't know what I envy most: her boyfriend or her metabolism.

Oh, who am I kidding? It will always be Brady.

No, I remind myself. *Things are going to change. Not tomorrow. Not in a month. Not in a year.*

Now.

38 DAYS AWAY

"What's the matter, *mija*?" Mom asks me for the six hundredth time since I came home from school this afternoon. "I wish you'd talk to me."

"Everything's fine," I lie while skimming the menu at The Pie Shoppe. I hate shutting her out, but I've been in a bad mood since I found out I got a D+ on the algebra homework I spent two hours on. I'm generally a pretty good student, except if you're talking about advanced algebra.

I'm also annoyed about Brady. Right when I decided that there was no time to waste and that I had to start making my move now . . . he disappeared. This happens every once in a while—he's a no-show at our meetings, I don't even see him in between classes. Last year I didn't talk to him for nearly an entire month, and any time I did see him he looked miserable. And I knew it was because of her. It had to be because of her. Because it was *always* about her. Brady's too much of a gentleman to confirm my suspicions, but there was only one subject he'd never confide in me about, and it was her.

What really stings right now is that Brady didn't even have the nerve to tell me directly he was missing our club meeting. He had Dan inform me that he had to take Parker somewhere.

Parker. Parker. Parker.

If *I* were with Brady, he wouldn't be at my beck and call. I wouldn't treat him like a private chauffeur. I wouldn't make him miss out on important things because I, unlike some people, don't think the world revolves around me.

So yeah, I'm officially down in the dumps, but since Mom's never one to let a bad mood ruin a night out, she presses. "How are things with Madelyn? Did she get the job at the record store? How was her chemistry exam? I know she was worried about it."

I didn't have the energy for her twenty questions. Mom's one of those moms who wants to know everything going on in everybody's life. She's that mom my friends like having around. They can tell her things they don't feel comfortable telling their own parents. I like that about her, but sometimes I don't want to have to talk about every little detail in my life or my friends'.

"Her exam went fine, but she hasn't heard about the job yet." I neglect to mention my homework grade, because Mom would call an emergency meeting with my teacher.

"Well, good news on the test. Poor thing about the job. How's she feeling? Should I text her?" Mom lifts her phone with a frown. "Although I don't like the fact she'd have to drive an hour each way for some job at a record store. It worries me."

While that's something reasonable to be worried about, my mom's also that mom who worries about anything and everything. And I do mean anything and everything.

It might seem nuts for Madelyn to apply for a weekend job in Akron, which is an hour away, but it's also the closest indie record store to our middle-of-nowhere Ohio town. There aren't many things she'll inconvenience herself for, but indie music and record stores are two of them.

"Should we get some breadsticks to tide us over until your father arrives?"

"Mom, you know I'm on a diet," I remind her.

"*Mi corazón,*" she says as she takes my hand. "I wish you realized beauty comes in all sizes. You are perfect the way you are. I never would've snatched your father up if I didn't have these curves." She winks at me and I want to vomit right here and now. Sometimes Mom talks to me like I'm her girlfriend and not her daughter. I don't want to know how she "snatched" my father.

"All I'm saying is you should be appreciative for the body you have." That's easy for her to say as she sits there in her skintight jeans and fitted shirt. Mom's curves are enviable, but her figure's an hourglass. Every curve is in the right place. (I'm sick to my stomach even thinking about Mom in these terms.) While I have Mom's honey-colored hair (although she highlights hers), sun-kissed skin (compliments of her Mexican ancestry), ample chest (the one thing Parker does *not* have), and big booty, I also have a stomach. There's this pooch below my belly button that won't go away. No matter how many crunches or diets I do. And I've done them all: I've counted points, cut out carbs (aka fun), ate for my blood type, and even went an entire week consuming nothing but cold-pressed juice. It would work for the first week, but then I'd plateau or get hungry (usually hungry). Maybe I should forget it and embrace that I'll never be a size four (or eight).

I remain silent. Mom isn't helping my mood.

I know, a caring mother who unconditionally loves her daughter—what a monster! But sometimes it can be too much. She never knows when to drop things.

"There are my girls!" Dad enters the pizzeria and sits down next to Mom. He plants a kiss on her cheek before giving my hand a squeeze. "How was everybody's day?"

"Mine was good," Mom says as she continues to study me. "Busy. Thanks for meeting us here. I couldn't even think about making dinner after dealing with the bake sale."

Mom's also a one-woman volunteer committee. If you need someone to sit on a board or raise funds, you call her. She used to only do it sporadically, but once I went to middle school, she wanted more things to do to fill her day, since additional kids were no longer an option.

"Any excuse to take my girls out," Dad replies as he loosens his tie.

"Hey, Phil!" a guy calls out across the restaurant.

Dad waves at him. "How's that new Explorer treating you, Bob?"

This is a common occurrence when we go out. My dad owns a car dealership. So he knows every car in town, where its owner got it, and which families refuse to buy American. (He always says that with a disapproving shake of his head.)

Waters are put in front of us and it takes me a second to place the voice asking us if we have any questions.

Parker.

This day has officially gotten worse. I didn't think that was possible, but anytime Parker enters the equation things often go from okay to excruciating.

"Hey, Hope," she says with a tight smile on her face that looks like it's causing her pain. "Hi, Mr. and Mrs. Kaplan. Great to see you."

I'm the only one at this table aware this friendly bit she's currently performing is solely for the benefit of my parents.

And, of course, Mom falls for it.

"Why, Parker!" Mom replies as if they're old friends. "I didn't know you worked here."

"Yep." Parker takes the pen that's behind her ear. "Can I start you off with something to drink?"

"I'm fine with water," I say.

"But, *mija*," Mom prods, "they have Cherry Coke here— that's your favorite."

Yeah, it is. But it's also full of calories.

"Sweetie, this isn't about that silly diet of yours, is it?" She sighs with a shake of her head.

Oh, no she didn't! Mom isn't seriously discussing my diet in front of Parker of all people?

"Fine. I'll have a Cherry Coke," I spit out before Mom does any more damage to my dwindling self-esteem. If my life were a video game, my self-worth would be flashing red right now.

"Do you want to start off with any appetizers?" Parker asks. "The mozzarella sticks are my favorite."

Oh my God! We get it, Parker, I scream inside my head. *You can eat whatever you want and have legs that are thinner than my arms.*

"We also have a new addition to our menu, where you can get a basket of four appetizers of your choice."

"Oh, that sounds delicious," Mom replies. "I know Hope will want her favorite: the cheesy bread."

I glare at her. "Mom, I'm not that hungry," I say even though I'm starving. Our club meeting went over because we still can't get the pulley to work, and we had one less member, thanks to Parker. So I haven't eaten since lunch, which is especially cruel because my lunch period is before eleven.

"You said in the car on the way here that you were starving." Mom glances at Dad. "Hope's in a mood."

"Mom," I scold her. This is so painful. Not to mention humiliating. I ball my hands into fists under the table, trying to keep it together.

"It makes me sick how much pressure you young girls deal with to be thin." Mom gives Parker a pat on the arm, as if she has any problems with her weight. It's girls like

Parker who make girls like me feel that pressure. "You know you don't have to please anybody but yourself. Right, girls?"

I seriously want to slide under the table and pretend like the last two minutes never happened. Parker looks as bored as ever, her pen poised, waiting to take our order. She even suppresses a yawn as if doing her job is inconveniencing her.

I can feel a simmer begin under my skin. I know that if my parents keep it up, I'm going to explode from rage and/or mortification. It's a toss-up at this point.

"Come on, kiddo!" Dad grabs my shoulder playfully. "Help your old man eat some cheesy appetizers!"

"Okay, fine!" I snap loudly. "Get the basket, okay? Why does everything have to be a big production? It's a stupid basket of food. God!"

Everybody at our table as well as the ones next to us stares at me.

Parker's mouth falls open a little. "Why don't I bring you your drinks and give you some more time with the menu?" She walks away quickly.

This is a disaster. Perfect Parker will no doubt tell everybody about my meltdown. By this time tomorrow, the entire school will be spreading rumors that I flipped over a table or something. Parker has all the power now because I couldn't control my temper.

So Parker wins, yet again.

I can feel tears burning in the back of my eyes. I will not, cannot, cry in front of Parker. Why did I think simply because I decided to make a change that something would happen? Yes, things have changed since yesterday, but for the worse: my near-failing grade, not seeing Brady, and now this.

"What on earth is going on with you today?" Mom asks, her voice low.

Now I feel even worse. Guilt overwhelms me as I see how concerned she is.

"Sorry," I say as I look down at the napkin in my lap. "I've had a really bad day and I'd prefer it if we didn't talk about my diet in front of strangers."

"Strangers?" Mom looks confused. "Parker is your friend."

It's sad how much Mom truly believes that. She lives in a world where her daughter's beautiful and perfect. A daughter who has all the friends in the world and everything she could ever want.

But here's the absolute truth: I'm miserable. I see what my parents have, that kind of love, and it's something I've always dreamed about. It's something I think I can have with Brady. He's all that I want, but I don't have him. I'm starting to feel like I never will.

What's worse is that it's my mom's fault I don't.

There was a brief period of time when Brady and I drifted apart.

Since he's a year older, he'd already been at the high school for a full year. At first, I didn't think anything would really change between us. Now I realize how naive I was.

We used to walk to middle school together every day. In that ten-minute walk, we'd catch up and talk. But once he was at the high school, the morning walks stopped. There weren't any opportunities to bump into each other between classes. I hardly saw him. He had new friends and after-school activities. Whenever I saw him that year, there were awkward pauses where there hadn't been any before. I didn't know the mundane details of his life, the ones that I used to relish.

It was during that yearlong gap when I realized my true feelings for Brady. We'd always been close, best friends and confidants. I guess there was always a part of me that had assumed we'd eventually end up together. We used to joke about getting married and having kids, but we were also seven at the time. It didn't mean anything.

It was on those lonely walks to school that I felt a part of me was missing. Anytime I saw him, I'd get this nervous, jittery feeling that was new to me. I didn't know what it all meant. When he told me about a girl he liked, I became jealous and instantly didn't like her. Then a voice popped into my head: *Why doesn't he like* me *that way?* I didn't want Brady to date anybody, because I liked him. But it was more than that. *We* were more than that.

At one point in that summer before my freshman year, I was coming from Madelyn's and Brady was outside his house mowing the front lawn. He looked up at me and smiled. It felt like my heart ripped itself out of my chest and went running straight to him. It was at that moment when I knew it wasn't some silly crush that was going to go away.

I loved Brady. Truly and deeply loved him. It wasn't some silly schoolgirl crush. It was real.

All I needed was for him to realize that all those other girls didn't matter. I was it. *Maybe now*, I told myself for the first time.

It made sense for us to officially become *us* now that we'd both be in high school together. Wasn't that the perfect time to start a relationship? We weren't kids anymore.

First, I needed Brady back in my life. We'd be starting school soon, where we could build our bond back. I knew it was only a matter of time.

Then Mom decided to throw a party.

Mom loves any excuse for a party. If she can make a theme out of it, we celebrate it. She also doesn't stick to the traditional holidays like Fourth of July, Thanksgiving, and New Year's. That's mere playtime for my mom. She throws bashes for Lincoln's birthday, Arbor Day, Earth Day, and, of course, Special Hope Days for when I lost my first tooth, aced a test, and, yes, even when I got my period for the first time. There's no occasion too small, private, or cringe-inducing to put her domestic skills to the test.

But when she said she was going to do an end-of-summer pool party to celebrate her "baby girl's entrance into high school," I loved the idea. Brady would come. We could start getting back to where we once were. And hopefully go beyond.

Mom had everything set. The only thing I had to worry about was whether or not Brady would show up.

But he did.

He made an automatic beeline for me as soon as he walked through the door. He had on a baggy T-shirt with his blue swimming trunks. Even though it was the end of summer, he was as pale as ever, courtesy of his summer job bagging groceries. While I'd spent most afternoons by our pool, so my skin soaked up the sun and I was darker. I also got a new black swimsuit with a push-up bra and "slimming technology" that I paired with a multicolored sarong to hide my more generous assets.

"Look who's a big bad freshman!" Brady said with a wink.

"Don't you forget it," I replied as I touched his forearm, keeping eye contact. (I had read a bunch of articles online on "How to Let Him Know You Like Him.")

His eyes scanned the room. "I don't know why I'm so shocked your mom has gone all-out."

The living room and outside pool area were decorated in colorful streamers and white fairy lights. Mom had decided on the theme of "fresh-Mex" since I was going to be a freshman, so the massive table in the dining room had a spread of guacamole, salsa, queso, tamales, pozole, mole, and enchiladas. Plus, a station where my dad was making virgin strawberry frozen margaritas.

"We know how to throw a party," I stated proudly. If there's a good reputation to have in our small town, being the kid whose parents host the best parties has to be up there. Pretty much every kid in my class and a few in Brady's were there. It wasn't that I was super popular, but I was liked enough.

"Can I show you something?" Brady asked, his eyes wide with excitement.

"Of course," I replied as I batted my eyelashes at him.

He pulled out his phone. "My buddy sent me this video and I've become obsessed. *Obsessed* all summer. I swear all I do is watch this stuff online."

I glanced at his screen as I started to watch this massive homemade contraption come to life. I tried to wrap my brain around it as a lever was pulled, then a crazy series of events unfolded, involving a mailbox, rotating gears, a bowling ball, a saw, a pool ball, a Coke can, oranges, helium canisters, and a ton of other items I couldn't keep track of, until something flew up and eventually cracked an egg. It took less than a minute.

It was insane.

"What is that?" I asked, trying to understand how it all worked.

"It's called a Rube Goldberg machine."

"Can we watch it again?"

"Of course!" Brady happily replayed it. "Can you imagine doing something like that?"

"I'm sure you could. It's all about proper placement or creating momentum." At least I assumed it was.

"I don't know. I'd probably trip and break something."

He had a valid point. Brady has many positive attributes, but being graceful and coordinated are not among them.

My mind went back to the machine. How one simple motion could cause a chain reaction.

I decided to test it out on us.

I stuck my hip out and nudged Brady. "I guess I should congratulate you."

"For what? Did I set some sort of geek record for amount of YouTube videos watched over the course of a summer?"

"No." I smiled at him, not only happy he was there, but that he wanted to share something so important with me. "That you get to resume spending each morning with me."

Brady laughed. "I know. Let me tell you something, it was a lonely freshman year."

"Well, I guess we have a lot to make up for." I took a step closer to him and noticed his eyes quickly glancing down to my chest, which had grown in the past year. It looked like momentum was going in my favor.

"Yes, we do." I could see his face begin to heat up.

I had a feeling this was it. The flirting had started, as it often did with us. But this time I was going to take it beyond flirting. I was going to be a girl of action.

"Thank goodness, we can be together again." I took another step, wanting to keep the forward motion going until I got my desired result. I placed my hand on his shoulder. "Like, really together."

Brady stammered a bit. He probably wasn't nearly as shocked at my boldness as I was. But this was my party. My time. I'd waited around long enough. It was going to happen. I could tell. The butterflies that took up residence anytime Brady was around me were now swirling so severely in my stomach, it was a miracle I could even stand.

He cleared his throat. "I, ah, could definitely get used to that idea."

I took that as the biggest green light in the history of teen flirting. I brushed myself against him. "Me too."

"Hope!" Mom came barreling toward us. "And, Brady, so good to see you, hon. I wanted to introduce you two to a new student joining you this year."

I hadn't even looked at the girl next to her because I was too busy scowling at Mom. I was so close to a *real* kiss with Brady. I could almost feel him on my lips.

I recalled Mom mentioning she'd met the new branch manager at the bank, who had a daughter who was going to be in my grade. She'd invited her to my party. I hadn't thought it was a big deal. Mom was also a one-woman welcome wagon.

When I finally stopped glaring at Mom, I looked at the new student: a cute girl with long, blond hair that nearly fell to her elbows. She had on a white tank, which showed a blue bikini underneath, paired with cut-off jean shorts. She had these pale blue eyes and freckles around her nose. She seemed harmless enough.

"This is Parker." Mom made introductions. "And this is my daughter, Hope, and her friend Brady."

"Hi, Parker!" Brady held out his hand. It was then I noticed the look on his face when he saw her. If I thought his face was red when I was flirting with him, it was practically crimson as he took in Parker for the first time.

"Hi," I said, my voice barely registering.

"Hope, your aunt is leaving—you need to come say good-bye." Mom practically dragged me out of the living room to the kitchen. I quickly stole a glance over my shoulder and saw Brady run his fingers through his hair as he talked to Parker. It was a nervous tic of his I'd only seen once before, when he asked Cynthia Madden out.

He stole a glance at me, too. Ran his fingers through his hair again.

I was so confused.

We had started something. It wasn't in my mind. He wanted it, too.

He gave me a sheepish smile before he turned his attention back to Parker. But there was a look in his eyes I couldn't quite place. It looked like regret.

Regret for what?

That we'd started?

That we'd stopped?

That he was talking to her instead of me?

These are questions I may never know the answers to.

I had no idea how long I was saying good-bye to my aunt or making small talk with my parents' friends. All I wanted to do was find Brady again. To pick up where we'd been before we were rudely interrupted.

Luckily, Madelyn came into the kitchen as my salvation.

"Hey, Gabriela!" Madelyn called out to my mom, who insists my friends call her by her first name. "Mind if I steal Hope so she can enjoy the pool portion of the pool party?"

Mom dismissed me as Madelyn, still clad head to toe in

black even though it was sweltering outside, guided me to the backyard. "Who's the new girl?"

My eyes went to the pool, where Parker was sitting on the steps in her bikini while Brady waded next to her. When he saw me, he waved me over. But I shook my head. He gave me a strange look, then gave up and dove underwater. When he emerged, Parker splashed him. They both laughed as if they were the ones who were lifelong friends.

"Her name is Parker," I replied, while what I wanted to say was that she was apparently going to be a problem.

Madelyn could sense me tense as I studied them, feeling helpless as I watched Brady start to slip further away from me. He had been so close. *We* had been so close. Then that girl had to show up and take him away from me.

But I wasn't going to go down without a fight.

"What are you going to do?"

I don't know why the thought popped immediately into my head, but it seemed so clear to me.

"Have you ever heard of a Rube Goldberg machine?"

36 DAYS AWAY

Brady makes it to our next meeting.

"Sorry for the other day, everybody," he says sheepishly as he enters the room. "Girl drama."

"Is there any other kind?" Dan jabs me in the ribs, while I push him away. Although it's nice for him to recognize I'm not just one of the guys. *This one time.*

"Everything okay?" I ask Brady as he puts his stuff down. As much as it would thrill me to hear that he and Parker are having problems, I don't like seeing him down.

Or maybe this is it. They've broken up and Brady is going to confess his true feelings for me.

Hey, crazier things have happened. My mom once went an entire day without sticking her nose into my business. Granted, she was bedridden with a horrible flu, but still, crazy.

"Yeah, Parker needed me to do something." He clenches his jaw.

"Oh, okay, it's just that we have a lot to do," I remind him. Then maybe he can remind Parker that we have a regional competition coming up. What could be so important that she couldn't find someone else to order around? Why can't Brady ever say no to her?

"I know, I know," he replies with a scowl, before heading to the table that houses our machine, leaving me behind.

Is he seriously mad at *me* now? I'm not the one taking him away from his commitments. I'm the one who had to work extra since he bailed on us because of her. But, of course, Parker can do no wrong in his eyes, while he has no trouble dismissing me.

What upsets me most is that all I want is to have an actual conversation with him. Sure, there's the flirting and bantering, but suddenly I feel like we haven't had an actual conversation about real things in a long time. It's either a trip down memory lane (which I always enjoy) or about the machine. Now when I ask him if there's anything wrong, he gives me the cold shoulder.

It used to be I could never get Brady to shut up about Parker. Those first few rides to high school were torture. First, he wanted to know everything I knew about Parker, which wasn't much. I knew she'd moved here from some Cincinnati suburb with her parents. I knew she had a sister in college. I'd overheard my mom tell my dad that Parker's dad worked at the bank and her mom was looking for a job. Oh yeah, and I also knew that her arrival had signified the utter destruction of my dreams. No big deal.

Every time he brought up Parker, I hoped he would at least acknowledge what had almost happened between the two of us. I was sick of being stuck in the friend zone with him. I had taken that step toward something more, but since then I'd been stuck in relationship purgatory. Waiting for Brady to finally realize that our time had come.

What was worse was that the way he was acting made me feel like it was a moment I had forced and he was too decent to embarrass me with the cold hard fact that we were permanently going to remain residents of Friendshipville, population: two.

Instead of focusing on us, all he wanted to talk about was her. How should he ask her out? Did I think she would say yes? I tried to keep his enthusiasm in check, saying I doubted anybody who recently moved to a new town would want a boyfriend right away. But my attempts at dissuading him only made him want her more.

Honestly, I didn't get it. She seemed pretty boring. Yeah, she was cute, but cute should only go so far. Plus, she wasn't even remotely friendly to me. It was because of me and my party that she even knew anybody at school.

With each conversation we had about Parker, I could feel him slipping away.

By the time they started dating, I learned to tune him out. It hurt too much to hear about how much he liked her—all I could hear was that he didn't like me. That he didn't see me the way he saw her. Sometimes after one of his Parker Is So Amazing monologues he'd look at me, realizing I was there, and I'd be forced to make some noise that could've been interpreted in myriad ways: approval, disapproval, annoyance, heartbreak.

I'd thought being in high school together was going to get us back to that place where the day didn't really start until we saw each other, where something didn't happen until we told each other about it. But he wasn't really there. Eventually, he got his driver's license and started taking Parker to school. He invited me to join them. My guess was that it was more out of obligation than desire. I turned him down. The human heart (and my self-esteem) could only take so much.

So I decided to start the Rube Goldberg Club. I doubt I'd ever see him if it weren't for our machines. It fuels my drive to make this one the best we can. I want us to win that competition in Cleveland. Then move on to nationals. I'm desperate to have something to show for our relationship. For there to be some public record of us. When I walk to and from class, I always glance at the glass cabinets that line the hallway, which are filled with pictures and trophies of championship teams. I want to be in one of those cases with Brady. To show that we did something while we were here. That we mattered, not simply because we won some award, but that we mattered to each other.

"Hope?" Dan calls out to me. "Do you plan on joining us or are you simply going to stare at the floor?"

I clear my throat. "Okay, let's see where we are."

We each go through and check every setting on our contraption. We finally got the mousetrap working yesterday. Now all we need is for the next twenty-two steps to fall into place.

I take the ball and place it on the ramp. It knocks over the dominos, which sets off the mousetrap. A surge of excitement takes over as we watch the pulley lever snap up a spoon, which holds a ball that goes flying and . . . misses the funnel by a hair.

"GAH!" I scream out.

Conor breaks his pencil in two, while Brady stomps on the floor, causing the table to rattle.

We're always so close, but never there.

"It's okay," Dan assures us. He pulls out a measuring tape and starts making calculations in his notebook. I always leave the heavy math-lifting to him. "I think we simply need to move the funnel an eighth of an inch over. We want the ball to hit the side so it rolls down for a while. It'll create a more dramatic effect than simply landing in the funnel."

It's always something.

I place my hands on my head, wondering if we're ever going to get this right. This is the one thing in my life I should have control over, but it's starting to feel like a hopeless cause. The first contraption we made my freshman year, an egg cracker, took us two weeks. It was a lot simpler, with only five steps. But each semester, we made a more complicated machine. This was the first year we decided to try for the regional competition, where we need at least twenty steps.

"Who would've thought this would be such a hard balloon to burst," Dan says with a snort.

"It's not like we haven't seen this done a million times online." I pout, because I'm frustrated. Not only at the machine, but at everything in my life. "It's a funnel. It's supposed to function like a funnel. All these items aren't doing what they're supposed to be doing."

Then it hits me: Maybe that's the problem. It isn't solely that we're using things we've seen in other contraptions online, but we're too focused on getting the balloon to inflate and then pop. We aren't having fun doing it. The whole purpose of a Rube Goldberg contraption is for it to have humor and whimsy. This machine is simply *meh*.

If we're going to have any chance at winning, we have to do better. We have to do more. Raise our game.

"This doesn't have any personality." I start examining every step of our machine.

"Yeah, it also doesn't work." Dan states the obvious.

"What's your favorite machine you've seen online?" I ask the group.

Conor stands up quickly. He tucks a strand of his chin-length straight black hair behind his ear. "That's easy—one that was *Lord of the Rings* themed, where it started by releasing a foot shaped like a Hobbit's and ended up with a ring being put on a finger. Hilarious, ingenuous, and stuck pretty close to its source material."

Dan looks thoughtful for a moment before he replies, "This may seem weird, but there was one that was a circus theme. Everything that moved had something Big Top–ish about it. It reminded me of going to the circus when I was little."

"We don't have any of those things," I reply with a defeated tone. "We need to add ourselves to it. Why have a regular needle pop the balloon if we can do something different?"

"Okay! Okay!" Brady practically jumps out of his seat. "I always thought it would be cool if we could have, like, I don't know, a medieval jouster on a horse stab the balloon with a lance instead of a needle."

"Oh!" Conor exclaims. "My grandpa used to tell me about this game they used to play in Manila, *Juego de Anillo*, where you'd ride a horse or a bike, holding a dagger to catch rings that would hang from a tree or something else. Maybe we could have the jouster stab through some rings, which would then pull a string to release another object. It would bring some rich culture to our project. Something you pasty white folks don't know anything about."

"I'm half-Mexican," I argue, although he has a point. We need to add more of us. More fun. More spice.

He bows down exaggeratedly to me. *"Lo siento, senorita."*

"I love it!" Brady holds up his hand to Conor for a high five. "We could have a damsel in distress behind the balloon so when it's popped, it's like we saved her."

"Ah, why does it have to be a girl that's in distress?" Even though I often do my gender a disservice by being so boy obsessed, I feel the need to stick up for females since I'm the only girl in the room.

The guys collectively roll their eyes at me.

"It's a theme," Conor says.

"It's also a lot of work," Dan admits.

How often do you get a second chance? That's what I really need right now, a second chance to prove . . . something. If not to Brady, then maybe to myself. Or both. We can make it better, make it fun, make it *us*.

It all comes back to Patience, Planning, and Perseverance.

"It is a lot of work," I concede. Then I look right at Brady and add, "But it would be worth it."

Brady studies me for a second, as if he's seeing me for the first time since he walked into the room. He curls his lip in a smile, nods, and says, "Let's get to work."

After we're done with some ridiculous and reinvigorating brainstorming, Brady walks me to my car. It's the first time in weeks we've been alone.

"Everything okay?" I ask one more time, hoping he'll open up to me now that it's just the two of us.

He nods. "Yeah, totally." He looks down at his phone, shutting me out once again.

I go through my mind trying to figure out what I could've done to make him so distant. Whenever Brady gets like this, I always think it's my fault. But maybe he's having a bad day. We're all allowed our off days. Or, in my case, weeks. Months. Possibly years.

He finally looks up. "Are we completely nuts for redoing the machine at this point?"

"Well, we're in a Rube Goldberg club, so clearly we don't have all our marbles," I tease. "But we can do it." I remind myself to stay positive. It's the only way we're going to survive.

"Yeah, we can." He pauses for a second. "Spending all this time with you reminds me of the old times. I'm really going to miss this next year. I'm really going to miss you, Hope."

And just like that, Brady does a one-eighty and knocks the wind from me. How am I supposed to react to that? Doesn't he realize how much those words mean to me? There are times I think everything between us is only in my mind, then he goes and says something that proves he also feels something between us.

I move ever so slightly, so I'm only a couple of inches from him as we walk out into the parking lot. He's brave enough to tell the truth, so I force myself to say the easiest confession. "I'm really going to miss you, too. I've known you my entire life."

He wraps his arm around me as a jolt of electricity ignites my entire body. "I know. I feel the same way."

But does he *truly* feel the same way?

He continues, "Luckily, I've got a few months left. And we've got this competition together. I know we can win. Remember, Hope: step by step. You've got this."

That's all I need from him, a glimmer of hope (sometimes my name is so spot-on). I know I'll hold on to this exchange when things seem dire. Although suddenly things seem to be looking up.

35 DAYS AWAY

The benefit of having Madelyn Austin as your best friend is that your weekends are anything but routine.

While most of our classmates are being predictable by going to the movies on a Saturday night, we're making our way into Chuck's, a small concert venue in Akron that allows sixteen-year-olds and up at certain shows. After we get our hands stamped to indicate we're minors, we head downstairs to the graffiti-covered basement, where the opening act, some band we've never heard of, is blasting the music so loud my chest vibrates.

Truth be told, we rarely know the bands we see, but it's better than sitting around our small town doing the same thing as everybody else. And, yes, this also prevents me from having to endure running into Brady and Parker as they hold hands, or catch them making out in the back of the movie theater.

The place is relatively empty, since the headliner isn't scheduled to go on until ten, when we'll already be on our way home. So we're two of the few people who actually listen and dance to the openers.

Well, Madelyn dances while I lean against the wall and bob my head up and down.

"Come on!" Madelyn grabs my hand to drag me to the sparse space in front of the stage.

"I'll get us drinks," I scream over a cover of an old Green Day song.

"You promised!" she shouts back. "We're going to have some fun, remember?"

Before I can respond, Madelyn runs right up to the front and begins to sing along, pump her fist, and dance like nobody's watching. I'm envious of how uninhibited she is. I wrap my arms around my tummy, wishing I hadn't picked such a tight-fitting shirt, as I make my way over to get us sodas. I squeeze between a couple that's sitting down at the bar. Not surprisingly, the tattoo-clad bartender ignores me, as he's busy chatting with two pretty girls. I pull out a twenty and hold it out on the bar, trying not to cringe when I notice how sticky the surface is. Madelyn found this place online during winter break and we've been the last two weeks, but it isn't the cleanest. Even though you haven't been able to smoke in bars for years in Ohio, the scent of cigarette smoke still lingers. (I got a nice lecture from Mom when she went to wash my jeans after our first visit, convinced I'd started smoking.)

The bartender helps the couple next to me and I hold out my twenty a bit farther, but he, once again, refuses to acknowledge my existence.

I've never been the kind of girl who guys notice. I've never been asked out on a date, unless you count going to homecoming every year with Madelyn. The only time guys go out of their way to talk to me is right before one of my parties. Or if I'm with my mom. There seems to be a twenty-foot radius of male admirers around Mom at any given moment.

Brady's the only guy who's ever *seen* me. He notices things like if I've gotten a new haircut. He compliments me, makes me feel like I matter. It's nice to have somebody besides my parents and Madelyn notice me.

Although Brady's done the opposite of noticing me today. Another day of avoidance. We had an emergency group meeting to discuss the new machine and Brady was a no-show. If he's so concerned about missing me next year, I would've thought he would put in more effort to be around me while we're still in the same town.

I can't make sense of it. How can someone I know so much about still puzzle me?

I feel a sting behind my eyes as I shake my head to try to get Brady and those all-too-familiar negative thoughts out. I'm here with Madelyn to enjoy the band, not feel sorry for myself.

Well, I'm also attempting to get drinks, but this bartender still refuses to acknowledge me and it's technically his *job* to notice people.

"Excuse me," I attempt to say over the music, but it's no use.

"Dude!" Madelyn appears by my side. "We need some refreshments, stat!"

The guy looks up and gives Madelyn a nod as she orders a Cherry Coke and a Shirley Temple. Last week when I placed the same order, I got a disapproving headshake. But he simply takes the money Madelyn has out, and she gives him a five-dollar tip, on top of a four-dollar tab.

"Madelyn!"

She shrugs. "That guarantees us he'll be more attentive next time."

But Madelyn is never one to leave mere disses alone. "Yo!" she calls out to the bartender, who approaches us again.

"Need anything else?" he asks. I have to hand it to her— he doesn't look at us with as much annoyance this time.

"Since we'll be regulars, I thought I'd give you the pleasure of meeting my awesome friend, Hope. I'm Madelyn. I know you meet a lot of people, but you won't have any problem remembering me once you see me dominate the dance floor."

The guy laughs. "Is that right?"

"You laugh now, but just you wait."

"You go to the U?"

He thinks we're in *college*?

"I wish. We have eighteen months left on our high school sentence. We live in Nowheresville. Have you heard of it?"

The guy nods. "It's right next to where I'm from, Desolation, USA."

I watch with envy as Madelyn continues to banter back and forth with this complete stranger. She's managed, within a couple of minutes, to turn this guy from finding us annoying to amusing. Well, Madelyn, at least.

He leans in closer. "You driving?"

Madelyn tilts her head toward me. "I've got my chauffeur right here."

"You want me to top off your drink with something stronger?"

I give her a warning look. My mom barely allows me to drive an hour to a concert, especially after I smelled like a chimney the first time. If Madelyn gets drunk, I'll never be able to leave the house again. Which, come to think of it, might be a dream come true for Mom. She'd always know where I was and there'd be no escape.

"Naw." Madelyn gives the guy a wink. "The only spirits I require are of the rock 'n' roll variety."

Right then, the band plays a cover of some '90s alternative song that Madelyn put on one of her Akron road-trip mixes. "Come on, Hope!" She pulls me by the hand—and since she's stronger than me, I'm in a losing battle. "You have to dance to this song. It's the best."

I reluctantly join Madelyn on the dance floor with my Cherry Coke. I shake my hips back and forth. It's not like I don't know how to dance, but I can't be like Madelyn.

"Hope!" she prods. "Let it go, have fun!"

I nod to get myself ready. I can do this. I've danced plenty of times around the house with my parents. We used to have dance parties when I was little. Mom would put on

Margarita or Selena and teach me *cumbia* dance moves, as well as a couple of Mexican folk routines. So I do know a thing or two about dancing.

But something holds me back. It's not like anybody's watching me, or if they are, they don't even know who I am. I just . . . can't.

"Hope!" Madelyn jumps up and down while she sings along at the top of her lungs.

You know what, Hope? the voice in my head screams. *Why the hell are you so concerned about these people and what they'll think of you? You'll never see them again.*

Well, I'll see some of them next week, but as I look around, nobody's even glancing at Madelyn. They're all doing their own thing. My head is right: I need to let loose, then maybe I'll get out of my funk. *Or* maybe I'll make a total fool out of myself.

Oh God, Hope, you're driving me crazy. Shut up and dance.

I close my eyes and join Madelyn, who *woots* with approval as I start to move to the beat of the drum. I shake, I shimmy, and I don't give a flying fig about what anybody around me thinks. Well, at least not over the next hour while I dance with Madelyn, who's ecstatic I've "finally gotten over" myself.

The band finishes and a few other people have started to crowd around us for the main band, but it's getting late, and since we need to make curfew, we head out. I'm still sweating as we head to my car, even though it's snowing outside.

"What got into you?" Madelyn asks once we get into the car. "Don't get me wrong—I love this side of you. I hope this becomes the norm, not the exception."

I shrug, even though I *am* pretty proud of myself for simply letting go. "I decided not to care."

"The world would be better off if we all decided to care a little less about the stuff that doesn't matter." Madelyn connects her phone to my stereo and puts on the mix she made for the hour drive back to Nowheresville. "Now we simply need to find you a new guy to obsess over and life will be wonderful."

I don't reply because this isn't the first (and I doubt it will be the last) time Madelyn's tried to get me to like a new guy. But I can't help how I feel. There hasn't been another guy. We're in a small town. The options are limited. Plus, it's really hard to have a crush on most of the guys in school when you've known them since kindergarten. There are some images that are hard to get out of your mind, like Josh Addison constantly digging for gold in his nose all through middle school or Joe Cooper getting his lunch freshly delivered (and hair combed and napkin put on his lap) by his mother every day at lunch until seventh grade. Even my mom thought that was too much.

What other guys are there? I haven't even entertained the *idea* of another guy. Should I? Brady has had years to develop feelings for me. What makes me think it'll magically happen in the next thirty-five days? He knows me better than he knows Parker. We always have a good time together, so I hate that it always comes down to this: *me.*

I can dance around and pretend to be happy for a couple of hours, but at the end of the day I'm not Parker.

Mom always tells me everything happens for a reason. Maybe there's a reason Brady and I aren't together, besides the fact he's obviously not attracted to me.

I can look at the cold, bitter facts, but my heart still wants what it wants.

Although, I can't forget about what happened yesterday. He had his arm around me. He admitted he was going to miss me.

Fact: You have to have some sort of feelings for someone in order to miss them. You don't miss somebody who doesn't mean anything to you. You don't miss a random neighbor or classmate.

I know I mean something to Brady.

"Hope?" Madelyn turns down the music. "Are you okay? You got quiet all of a sudden. What happened to outgoing, doesn't-give-a-crap Hope? She was just here!" Madelyn pretends to look in the backseat of the car and the glove compartment. "Where did she go? Hello? Hello?"

"I'm still here," I reply, but that's not true. I do give a crap. That sense of lightness and joy I had moments ago has disappeared. Sure, it was fun to dance around without a care in the world, but an hour of bliss can't fix everything.

"Good, I think we should look at their calendar and see if we can pull off coming at least once during the week. I know Gabriela will probably have a coronary about you going out on a school night, but we need more of this in our lives. What about Wednesday? Music is the perfect antidote for hump day."

"Well, we have to redo the machine so during the week is going to be tough," I remind her.

"Right." She sits back in her seat with her arms folded. I know she's annoyed I can't simply drop everything and go to concerts every night of the week, but I made a commitment to the team.

Madelyn sighs. "Man, I already miss Fun Hope."

Me too.

33 DAYS AWAY

The concert feels like two years ago, not two days. Instead of feeling free, all I feel now is pressure. Being around Brady isn't even giving me any comfort.

"You're a lifesaver," he tells me as the club takes over the downstairs TV room in my house. We've moved the machine here, since the changes are going to take a lot more time than a couple of hours each week in Mr. Sutton's classroom.

Our large downstairs (couch and TV on one end and Mom's gym equipment on the other) has been transformed into a basement of misfit toy scraps. LEGOs, ramps, strings, dominos, plastic funnels, and other random items we think we may need are scattered all over the floor and every surface.

"We need the space and the extra hours to get this right," I say. I spent Sunday mapping out all the changes we need to make and items we need to buy. Dan and Conor are busy in the corner organizing our new elements. I look back at Brady. I didn't see him all weekend, which isn't anything new since Parker, but even today at school he was still a little distant. I try to bring him back to me. "Plus, if this machine doesn't work, I'll have to rely on my foolproof backup plan of becoming a professional bowler."

"Huh?" He looks at me distractedly. "Sorry, I was somewhere else."

It seems like lately his thoughts are always on *someone* else.

But maybe it's just the stress of the upcoming competition. I try again: "Hey, you've been a little distant lately. Anything you want to talk about? Is it the club?"

Brady looks at me for a beat longer than normal. "No, no, everything with the club is cool. It's just . . ."

He lets his uncertainty linger in the air. I don't want to push, but I know him. Something is bothering him. He wants to tell me.

I take a step so we are only inches apart. "Brady, it's me. You can tell me anything." Or at least he used to.

He nods to himself. "Yeah, so here's the thing . . ."

I lean even closer into him. This is it. The confession I've been waiting for. There's a problem with Parker.

"Yes?" I ask, trying to not appear so desperate.

"Yeah," he says as he takes a giant step away from me. "I can't believe I've been in your house for like ten minutes and your mom hasn't gone into hostess mode."

As if she were summoned (or eavesdropping), Mom calls down, "I'm bringing down some refreshments!"

"Nice, all is well with the world," Brady says before abruptly turning around to head toward Dan and Conor, leaving me there alone and utterly speechless.

Nothing is well in my world.

At this rate, I'll have every hair on the back of Brady's head memorized soon, since all I see of him anymore is when he turns away from me.

Mom appears at the bottom of the stairs with a tray of snacks: chips with her homemade salsa, sandwiches, grapes, and assorted beverages. She's excited, as always, to be in the thick of it.

The guys jump up with gratitude as they begin devouring the food. I take a sparkling water and a handful of grapes. "Thanks, Mom."

"Oh, what's this for?" She picks up a pulley system we rigged that will hopefully get a cannon to fire a ball that will hit a target that will launch a ship across a moat.

Dan begins to explain the system in detailed and complex mathematical terms. Mom appears enthralled, while I start to zone out. I'm able to look at our machines and see what needs to get done, but I can't necessarily explain the whys of it in degrees and centrifugal force.

"That's fascinating." Mom's eyes are wide as she takes in the mess we've made of her basement. "Don't mind me. I know you guys have a lot of work to do."

Conor's in the corner fiddling with a fan, and notices us looking at the room with fear, dread, and uncertainty.

"It's the job that's never started as takes the longest to finish," he says in a serious tone.

"Why that's very wise of you, Conor."

"Um, Mrs. Kaplan, that's Tolkien."

"Who?"

Conor looks as if he's been slapped in the face. "He's only one of the greatest novelists of all time! *The Hobbit*? *The Lord of the Rings*?" He's searching my mom for some sort of recognition.

"Oh yes, I remember seeing one of those movies on TV once." Mom shrugs an apology to Conor, whose mouth's open in shock. Or disgust. "And, hon, it's Gabriela, please."

Conor shakes his head violently at the thought of calling anybody's parent by their first name.

"Well, I guess I should get going and leave you geniuses to it. Let me know if you need anything." She gives us her biggest smile before retreating upstairs.

"Okay!" I get the group's focus back to our task at hand and away from the stairs. I break down everything that needs to happen and how best to tackle it. I attempt a schedule to keep us ahead of the game.

It's remarkable how something so easy in theory can be so complicated in practice.

25 DAYS AWAY

"Thank you for gracing me with your presence," Madelyn remarks dryly, the following Tuesday at lunch. She refuses to look up from her food. "So is this what I should expect *if* you and Brady ever get together: a one-way ticket to friend-dumpsville?"

"This machine is taking up all of our time, I swear." It really is. Mr. Sutton's free during our lunch period, so we've been spending the last week's lunches going through each of our new parts and brainstorming.

"I have a feeling I'm seeing the new norm from you." She starts scraping the black fingernail polish off her thumb with her pointer finger. It's something she does when she's nervous or irritated. If I were a betting person, I'd put all my money on the latter. "I've already resigned myself to the fact that we're a continuingly failing Bechdel test. Heaven forbid we have a conversation that doesn't revolve around Brady, but now I never get to see you because of Brady."

"Wait." I'm confused. "What test?"

She sighs as if I asked her what one plus one equals. "Well, it's used to assess a work of fiction, not real life, but it's a test to see if two female characters have a conversation about something other than a guy. After I read about it the other week, I started to notice that all we do is talk about guys. Well, one guy in particular. *If* you even bother to make time for me lately. Then any time I try to mention a new band I've discovered, you start wondering if Brady would like them, and if they came nearby in concert, if you could get Brady to go without Parker."

"I'm sorry, but I'm not talking about Brady right now—this is about the machine." My whole life this past week has been all about the machine. Yes, Brady is a part of that, but despite what Madelyn thinks not everything is about him. I've put so much blood (from scraping my hand against a nail), sweat (putting together that LEGO castle was no joke), and tears (seriously, the LEGO castle almost destroyed me) into this machine, I have to see it through.

"HA!" she says so loudly the table next to us turns around. It's pretty clear she doesn't find any of this funny. "Like your machines aren't all about Brady."

While it's true the club started because of him, I really do enjoy working on the machines. Next year, after Brady's at college, I'll still be as involved in the club. It's Dan who'll be the hardest to replace.

"The club's really important to me. You know that. I've invested so much into it. We have less than four weeks to pull this off, and if we do, we're practically guaranteed to move on to nationals." I've already explained this to her, when I had to cancel our weekly concert outing last Saturday.

"Again, I'm really sorry." I nudge her foot under the table in hopes that she will at least look at me. Madelyn can hold a grudge, so I want to get back in her good graces as fast as humanly possible. "After the competition, we'll go dancing and to concerts all the time. But for now, no more talk about the B-word, unless it's a band."

She isn't budging, so I continue, "We haven't named the machine yet, what if we called it the Madelynator?"

A slight smile cracks her face. She finally looks up at me. "I thought you said the machine made a balloon pop, not that it made awesome."

"My bad." I wink at her. "So what's been going on with you?"

"Besides having rock stars wanting to be *my* groupies?"

"Obviously." I'm relieved things are getting back to normal. Plus, I need to prove to her, and maybe more to myself, that I can go an entire lunch period without talking about the henceforth-banned B-word.

I never wanted to be one of those girls whose entire life revolved around a boy, so sometimes when I step away from myself and see how desperate I've become it makes me ashamed.

My head and heart really need to find some sort of compromise.

"Mi corazón!" Mom greets me after school before I even have the front door entirely open. "How was your day? How were classes? How's Madelyn?"

My initial urge is to be agitated at her constant bombardment, but I stop myself.

"It was good," I reply as I take off my coat. It suddenly hits me that the house smells of freshly baked cookies. "Smells amazing in here, Mom."

"I'm glad you think so." She pats the seat next to her on the large V-shaped sectional couch in the living room. "I made them for you."

There's a plate of my favorite cookies, double-fudge chunk, on the coffee table with a glass of milk. Mom's constantly making cookies for bake sales and school events. While she always saves some for Dad and me, there's only one reason Mom would make a batch solely for me: something's wrong.

"What's going on?" I feel a knot form in my stomach. "Is everything okay with Grandma?"

"Yes, of course." Mom hands me a piece of paper as I sit down. It's from my math teacher. I scored a sixty-four on the last exam. To be honest, I'm pretty pleased I got more questions right than wrong. "I had a conversation with Ms. Porter about your progress in class."

More like lack of progress.

"If you don't start getting *at least* a C plus or higher on the three remaining tests this semester, you'll fail and have to repeat the class next year."

There's a buzzing noise in my ears when I hear the word *repeat*. There's no way I can go through this again.

Mom continues as she begins to rub my back. "So you're going to work with a tutor immediately, starting tomorrow."

"Okay." I resign myself. I'm horrified at the thought of having a tutor, since it means one of my classmates will know how absolutely idiotic I am, but I really don't have a choice. That's a better option than the entire school knowing I have to repeat a class.

"So, I've spoken with Parker—"

"WHAT!" I scream. "You don't mean *Parker Jackson* is going to be my tutor?"

Mom looks genuinely shocked. "What's the problem with Parker?"

Seriously? Where do I even begin?

Mom goes on. "Ms. Porter highly recommends her. She has experience tutoring in algebra and had a ninety-eight average on her exams last year. We're fortunate she's able to fit us in three times a week."

"THREE TIMES A WEEK?" I can't help but shriek back everything she's saying. I refuse to believe it. I have to come up with something. "But what about the machine? We have so much work to do before regionals."

Mom waves her hand dismissively. "You can work on the machine after your tutoring sessions are over. There are three other people who can cover for you. This is more important. We will work around Parker's schedule—she's very busy with her job at The Pie Shoppe."

Yes, what a saint. We don't want to inconvenience Parker, do we? It's not as if she's doing this out of the goodness of her heart. She's going to get paid.

I wouldn't put it past her to sabotage me so I fail.

There's no way I can tolerate one tutoring session with her, much less three a week for the rest of the year.

I decide to go for broke. "Mom, can we talk to Dan instead? He's ridiculously smart. Or anybody else? I'd really prefer it not be Parker."

Mom shakes her head. "You're being silly. Why wouldn't you want Parker? She's the sweetest little thing. Besides, it's a done deal."

"*Mom—,*" I protest.

"Enough!" She snaps. Mom rarely loses her temper with me. So when she does, it's terrifying. "I don't want to hear another word about this, Hope. You're not failing a class, period. You're going to meet when it works for Parker. I will not let extracurricular activities get in the way of school. I will not let you mess up your chance for a good college by being stubborn. I'm not having this conversation again. Have I made myself clear?"

All I can do is nod. She has made herself crystal clear.

I'm at Parker's mercy.

I fight back the tears stinging behind my eyes.

Mom's face softens. "Sweetie, I'm sorry I raised my voice, but I need to do what's best for you."

It's hopeless. I shove a cookie into my mouth. It's soft and gooey, and exactly what I need.

A memory flashes into my head of when I was little. Brady would come over after school if his mom was working late. There'd be napkins on the kitchen table with our names written on them, and the fresh cookies Mom used to make whenever I'd have someone over. Brady used to spend the day at school guessing which cookie it would be. Anytime we passed each other in the hallway, he'd say a different kind. I'd start to giggle even before he reached me. He always started with the basics—chocolate chip, oatmeal raisin—and then by the afternoon he'd start making up insane flavors. (Chocolate ant pistachio fig being my personal favorite of his made-up ones.)

"See, I knew a cookie would make you smile." Mom brushes my cheek lightly with her thumb.

But, of course, it isn't the cookie that did that.

"I have a surprise for you!" I say to Brady as he arrives at his locker the next morning. I keep my right arm behind my back, concealing the cookies I've wrapped in a napkin with his name on it. That burst of nostalgia alone should score me some extra points.

He gives me that crooked smile of his. "Did you figure out the pulley system?"

"No. It's something very, very sweet."

"Ah, you discovered a way our machine can make chocolate as well as pop a balloon?" He scratches his head, making his hair even messier.

"No." I bite my lip flirtatiously. "Guess again."

He laughs a little. "Well, now all I'm thinking about is chocolate."

"You almost got it!" I bounce on my tiptoes so I'm closer to him. I nudge him playfully. "You know, I should make you close your eyes as I'm about to take you on a journey down memory lane."

He folds his arms. His eyes squint suspiciously. "Are you going to throw a pie in my face again?"

"That was not my fault!" I protest, but I can't help but smile as the memory surfaces. Thrilled he remembers it, even if he's besmirching my reputation.

It was the summer I turned eleven. Mom hosted an ice-cream social as a fundraiser for the nursing home. Brady and I were in charge of bringing new pies to the table where they were being served. I turned around with a pie, right as

Brady, graceful as ever, tripped on the rug. His face landed right in the pie.

I can no longer contain my laughter as I picture his bewildered expression as he wiped cherry filling from his glasses.

"Yeah, yeah, yeah." He shakes his head. "You had impeccable timing. You probably put the rug there."

"Well, here!" I proudly hand him the cookies. "Consider it a peace offering. Five years later."

His eyes light up as he begins to unwrap the napkin. "Aw man, your mom makes the best cookies." Despite the early hour, he happily takes a huge bite. "You know, I think this much-needed apology has probably accrued some interest. I'm going to need many, many more cookies to even begin to emotionally recover from that humiliation."

"I'll see what I can do."

See, Brady? I think to myself. *See how easy things are with us? How come it can't always be like this? How come you can't pick me?*

"Babe!" Brady says, and my stomach flutters for a brief second. But a quick look over my shoulder confirms the truth: He's talking to Parker.

Parker, the reason things can't be like this between us. He has her. He chose her.

She approaches us cautiously with her normal tight smile on her face. I try to keep my face neutral and suppress the murderous rage growing inside me. I can't believe I have to spend an hour with her after school today. Even thinking about it causes a pain in my stomach. I don't want to know if Brady's aware of my horrible grades and how his perfect, angelic girlfriend's going to save me.

"Babe," Brady continues, oblivious to this awkward situation. "You've got to try one of the cookies Hope's mom made."

To my horror, he hands her a cookie. She gives him a little smile as she takes a bite. She begins nodding. "So good," she says to him as she covers her mouth. Finally, she turns to me and deigns to acknowledge my existence. "Thanks, Hope."

I stand there dumbfounded as I watch her greedily eat an entire cookie before eight o'clock in the morning.

I'm so tired of this.

"Well, I better get to class," I say between clenched teeth. I force a smile as Brady thanks me again before I walk away.

I try to remind myself that I have a Plan. That I will eventually Persevere with a little bit more Patience.

But at this moment I don't want to think about that. I hate, absolutely *hate* that I have to rely on Parker for anything. That the only way I have a chance to pass is because of her. I don't want to owe her anything, to be beholden to her.

Parker has everything, while I'm desperately holding on to the little I do have.

Parker

479 DAYS LEFT

I don't see the point of looking into the past.

Why would I? There are way too many bad memories that lie in its ruins.

All I want to do is look ahead. I'll get out of here, go to college, and hopefully forget everything that's happened in the past year.

While there isn't much I can do about the family I was born into, I do realize how lucky I am to have the friends I have and, of course, to be with Brady.

"You working tonight?" he asks as he pulls into the school parking lot, his right hand lightly resting on my knee.

"Yes, from six to ten. I also have a tutoring session after school." I don't know if I should mention I'm tutoring Hope. There's a good chance she's going to tell him, but it isn't my place to divulge her academic issues.

"Do you need a ride?"

"I don't think so." Hope's mom called last night to inform me that Hope is going to take us to her house after school. I figure I could ask her mom for a ride to The Pie Shoppe or, worst case, walk. It's only two miles away. "I'll call you if I need one tonight."

I hate that I have to rely on Brady and my friends to drive me around. Brady always tells me it's okay, but then I overhear him canceling plans. He's had to miss his Rube Goldberg club meetings because of me. Not as if Hope needs any more reason to hate me.

It's not fair that Brady has to rearrange his life because of me, although my situation isn't fair to me either.

Brady puts his arm around me like always as we walk into school and down the hallway. He's so much taller than me. I fit perfectly in the crook of his arm. He's become a security blanket with his body and weight somehow protecting me.

I know I only have a few months left with him here to help me. I'm not deluding myself into thinking we're going to last beyond high school. Brady's going to Purdue, in Indiana, for engineering in the fall. I won't have the resources to visit him.

Even though I know we aren't destined for forever, I'm going to enjoy my time with him as long as I can.

"I'll be a minute." I give him a quick kiss before going to my locker. Even walking down the hallway by myself, I feel exposed.

I quickly grab my notebook out of my locker and head to Brady's. When I turn the corner, I freeze. Hope is at his locker. She's bouncing up and down, touching his arm, and throwing her head back while she laughs. I take a step back, wondering how much I'd upset Brady if I ditched him. We always walk together to our first class, but I don't want to deal with Hope.

I start to turn when Brady catches my eye. "Babe!" he shouts with a grin on his face.

Hope looks over her shoulder and I can practically see steam coming out of her ears. I know I have to go over there. I slowly walk to them with as much of a smile as I can muster.

"Babe, you've got to try one of the cookies Hope's mom made." Brady hands me a huge cookie that's bursting with chocolate chunks. While it's only a cookie, I feel so grateful. I give Brady a smile before I take a bite. I didn't work last night and ate most of my lunch yesterday, so I haven't eaten in nearly eighteen hours.

"So good," I say to Hope while I cover my mouth, embarrassed with how much I've shoved into it. She refuses to even look at me. "Thanks, Hope."

I try to savor every morsel. As much as I want to inhale the whole thing, I know all too well that I'll cramp up if I introduce food too quickly into my empty stomach.

Hope's glaring at the ground. I don't know if she's embarrassed I'm going to tutor her or if she's mad at something else. Hope always seems like she's mad at the whole world . . . except for Brady. She's always roses and sunshine around him.

Hope clenches her jaw. "Well, I better get to class." She turns on her heel quickly as Brady and I thank her again.

"Do you want another one?" he asks, holding out a cookie. "Did you eat dinner last night?"

"I'm okay," I lie. I hate being a charity case.

"I guess we better head to class." He shuts his locker, then puts his arm around me as we walk. We reach the point in the hallway where we have to part for our first class. "See you at lunch," he says to me, then kisses me lightly on the lips. "Unless, of course, I'm lucky enough to run into you sooner."

"The luck, Mr. Lambert, would be all mine." I give his hand a squeeze before I walk away.

Lunch. I've come to dread lunch period, which is ironic since it's truly my biggest lifeline. Brady, Lila, and my other friends who know the truth always offer to buy me lunch, but they've done so much already. So I take my tray and ignore the looks of pity from the lunch workers and the stares from my classmates as I fill my tray up with as much food as I can to sustain me until the next day.

What other choice do I have?

If it wasn't for the school lunch program, I'd starve.

It's hard to keep a secret in a small town.

I still don't fully understand how mine has been contained for so long. While several of the adults in town know what happened, I think they mostly feel sorry for me, since none of it was my fault, and have kept quiet. Of course, my closest friends know. It'd be nearly impossible for them not to.

I have to constantly remind myself who knows and who doesn't. It's tiring being two different people. It's not as if I'm not me, but I have to be on guard. Careful of what I say and to whom. It's more out of pride than anything else that I don't want people to know. It's hard enough being in high school without giving people a reason to torment you or, worse, pity you. There are some people I have to watch myself around more than others. Hope Kaplan is a perfect example of someone I have to be careful about. Especially since Hope despises me because she's in love with Brady.

It's almost laughable that she thinks it's a secret. I kind of feel sorry for her that she doesn't realize he sees her only as a friend. They simply don't have the kind of connection he and I do. So she takes it out on me.

I wanted to turn down Ms. Porter when she asked me to tutor Hope, but I need the money. Plus, her mom has been really great since everything fell apart. I was convinced Hope knew everything, but her mom assured me my secret was safe with her.

I trust Mrs. Kaplan. It's everybody else I'm worried about.

There's a knot in my stomach as I approach Hope after school. It twists deeper when I see Hope's best friend, Madelyn, waiting with her. Madelyn's one of those intimidating people who can ruin your day with a look. It's pretty obvious she's not a fan of mine. She glares at me as I make my way toward them. Then Madelyn leans in and whispers something in Hope's ear, which results in a hearty laugh from Hope. It doesn't take a genius to know the target of the comment.

"Hi, guys," I say hesitantly. "Are you ready, Hope?"

Hope slams her locker shut. "Of course, Parker. If you're ready, then I'm ready. I'm at your command."

I try to ignore the disdain in her voice.

We walk to her car without speaking a single word to

each other. I try to figure out if there's anything I can say that won't aggravate her further. I can't mention Brady, even though he's a favorite topic of hers. Her Rube Goldberg machines are also off-limits because of Brady. I don't want to start talking to her about algebra, since she probably already feels put out that I'm her tutor.

Hope has two sides to her: the fun, carefree side that Brady talks about and then the bitter, angry one I encounter on an almost daily basis.

For nearly my entire first year here, I wanted to be friends with her. Brady still wants that for us, but it's more than apparent Hope isn't interested in being friends with me. She doesn't even want to be in the same room as me, so it's beyond awkward when we both get into her shiny new red car.

After a couple more minutes of not speaking, I decide I can't take it anymore. "I really like this song," I say. "I don't think I've heard it before—who is it?"

"It's nobody," she replies coldly before switching to another song.

Luckily, it's only a few minutes until we reach her house.

"Hope, *mija*, is Parker with you?" her mom calls out as we enter.

"Yes," Hope replies with the right amount of dread to make me not feel welcomed.

"Parker!" Mrs. Kaplan greets me with a hug. "Thank you so much for coming, hon. I figured the dining room table would be the best place for you two to work. I also whipped up a few snacks for you."

It's strange to be in this house when it isn't packed with

people and decorated for a special occasion. We enter the dining room. At the head of its large oak table, Mrs. Kaplan has set down platters filled with apple slices and peanut butter, potato chips and dip, and brownies.

"This is amazing—thank you so much, Mrs. Kaplan." I resist the urge to start eating right away. I want to take Hope's lead. She always gets weird about food when I'm around.

I'm pretty certain Hope thinks she's fat. She is not. She has curves I would love to have. To me, curves symbolize a strong, healthy body. I'm the opposite. I've always been thin, but now I'm skinny. While Hope probably envies my size, it's not something to be proud of.

"Now, Parker, I've repeatedly told you to call me Gabriela." Mrs. Kaplan wraps an arm around me.

"Sorry," I reply, although I always feel uncomfortable calling adults by their first name. I'll try to find a way not to call her by any name if I can help it.

"Nothing to be sorry for." She pats my hand. "Now eat! And be mathematical geniuses!" She gives us a big smile before she leaves us alone.

I sit down at the table, pull out my books, and take an apple slice and bite into it, ignoring Hope's glare from across the table.

"So I think we should start with last week's exam," I say as I pull out a copy of Hope's test. "We can go through each equation and talk through it. I find it best to verbalize these problems."

"I'm not stupid," Hope interrupts me. She's looking down at the table.

"Nobody thinks you're—"

"Please," she practically spits at me. "I can't figure out this stuff, okay? So I guess I'm an idiot."

"Hope, you are *not* stupid," I insist. Still, she refuses to look up. I start circling a few equations on the paper and slide it over. "You got these correct. So you have the basics down. The ones you didn't, you were usually only one calculation away from getting it right. You were really close."

Her gaze is now on the paper, but I can't tell if she's hearing me.

I continue, "You know your machines? You sometimes have trouble with a certain step because a ramp is slightly off or something wasn't calibrated correctly, right?"

She gives me a tiny nod.

"Well, that's exactly what's going on here. You're on the right track, but we have to make a slight adjustment. You understand what needs to be done to solve the problem, but there's a variable that needs to be recalculated. Once we get that down, there won't be an algebraic egg you can't crack." My lame attempt at humor actually makes her lips move up ever so slightly. "Let's tackle this first one, okay?"

She finally looks up. "Okay."

"Great!" I move my chair so we're closer together and I'm within an arm's reach of the food.

"Oh, sweeties!" Hope's mom comes into the room. "I forgot to offer you something to drink! What was I thinking?"

"God, Mom!" Hope snaps at her. "We're trying to work! Can you let us do that?"

Hope's mom backs away. "Yes, of course. Why don't I bring some water and sodas for you? Then I promise to be out of your hair."

"That would be great," I reply, much to Hope's frustration. "Thanks so much."

"Fine," Hope grunts. She takes a deep breath and shakes her head.

I want to shake Hope. She always seems annoyed by her mother. Or embarrassed by her. I don't understand it. Her mom got her a tutor. Her mom made us a snack and simply wants to get us something to drink. What's wrong with that?

Plus, her mom is here. One of the simplest tasks for any parent: being there for their child. Hope's mom may be clingy, but it's better than having a neglectful mother.

Sure, I have the boyfriend, but Hope has a family. She has security. She has everything that truly matters.

The problem with tutoring Hope before work is that it makes it difficult for me to find my own time to study. Sometimes The Pie Shoppe isn't that busy, and I can squeeze in homework between tables, but I'm not so fortunate tonight.

The benefits of it being busy are that I make extra money in tips, and the time flies. It feels as if I've only been here for an hour when the door opens a little after ten and Brady comes in.

"How'd it go tonight?" he asks.

I'm clearing a corner table littered with beer bottles that have been emptied by a group of guys getting off work at the plastic plant on the outskirts of town. It was your basic late-night group: drunk and rowdy . . . and incredibly stingy with their tips.

I give Brady a small smile as I pocket the two dollars in change they left on a forty-dollar tab. "Fine. I'll be a second."

As I grab my bag from the back and say good-bye to my boss, I quickly count all my tips and am happy to have nearly forty dollars for the evening. I shove twelve dollars in my pocket and put the rest in the money belt I hide underneath my clothes. I plan on making my weekly deposit to my "private bank" on the weekend.

The cold February air shocks us as we step outside. I bundle up under my jacket, dreading what's waiting for me at home.

Home.

It's incredible all that word encompasses. Home used to mean a three-bedroom, split-level ranch with a backyard, a washing machine, a dryer, and central air.

As Brady pulls up to the trailer I now share with my sister, I still can't believe how far I've fallen.

There are few people who know where I really live. When I stop to think about it, it's strange how little I know about the home lives of most of my classmates. Of course, there are people like Hope, whose parents are a big part of the community and constantly host parties at their house. But my parents never made a big impression at school or in the community. They never met my teachers, mostly because I never gave them a reason to. They kept to themselves. When they both decided to disappear, no one really noticed. To most people, they'd never existed to begin with.

"You going to be okay?" Brady asks as he looks at the darkened trailer.

"Yes," I say, although I'm not so sure. It's quiet now. With any luck, I'll be asleep by the time Hayley comes home from the bar, and she'll be alone.

Brady looks around at the dozens of other trailers next to ours. "You know you can always stay the night with me if you want."

It's something I often do. On the weekends, I stay at Lila's house. If things get bad with Hayley, I'll either crash with her or Brady. While it's tempting, I have tests to study for and there's no way I'd get the work done if I went to his house.

"I'm fine," I assure him. "Thanks for the ride. I really appreciate it."

He grimaces. "Babe, what do I always tell you?"

"I know, I know." Brady is always reminding me that I don't have to thank him every time he gives me a ride or pays for things. "That's what boyfriends do" is his automatic response. Not the boyfriends of other girls. Sure, the guys might pay for things or drive a girl somewhere, but those girls could survive without it.

I couldn't.

"Well, I'll see you tomorrow." I lean in to kiss him. He places his hand on the side of my face and draws me in even closer. I can tell I smell like the pizza place. I'm never able to wear the same clothes to work as school.

After a few minutes, we pull away. Brady waits to make sure I'm safely inside the trailer before he drives off.

I shiver at how cold it is inside. I place the twelve dollars on the counter, knowing Hayley will believe it was a slow Wednesday night. It's harder to keep money from her on the weekends.

I know it wasn't fair to my sister that she had to leave college to parent me. I chip in as much as I can, but I need to save some money for myself. I need an escape plan. As I look at the empty cigarette box and vodka bottle on the counter, it's clear my hard-earned money isn't being well spent. I hate that Hayley has already given up.

My older sister is a cautionary tale for me. There are times when I want to scream at her to fight and to become something more. She can't let what our parents did to us ruin her. But I often fear I'm too late.

I place her empties in the trash, take a quick, tepid shower, study, and then spread my sleeping bag onto the couch and slip inside.

I say a silent thank-you to the universe that I've survived another day, knowing tomorrow will bring its own challenges. I don't care. Tomorrow means I'm one day closer to graduation. One day closer to finally being able to leave this place and this life behind.

478 DAYS LEFT

Nothing tests a friendship like a good old family scandal.

I met my best friend, Lila, at the same party where I met Brady, a couple of days after we moved to town. Brady introduced me around to people and instantly made me feel welcomed. Lila brought me into her tight circle of friends and we've been inseparable since.

"Have you and Brady talked about Valentine's yet?" Lila asks the next morning between classes.

"Not really. I have to work that night." Valentine's Day is next week and I'm dreading it. I can't afford to give Brady a present, and while I know he won't expect anything, I hate always being the moocher. "Plus, he probably has to work on the machine anyway."

I love that Brady has something like the Rube Goldberg club to keep him occupied. Not only are the machines really cool, but I don't feel as if I'm neglecting him when I have to work so much.

"Oh, you know Hope will find some way to keep him tethered to her that day." Lila's black curls bounce back and forth as she shakes her head.

I shrug, since she's absolutely right. "I know, but they really have a lot to do."

"Are you sure you're okay with him being with her in Cleveland all by himself? I don't trust that girl."

"First, they won't be all by themselves. And second, I trust Brady." I do. If he wanted to be with Hope, he would've been with her. It's not like he hasn't had plenty of opportunities.

"We should totally road trip!" she offers. "It's only a two-hour drive. We can go and support him."

"I really need the weekend shifts."

It's a common reply from me. There are so many parties and other events I can't attend because I always have to work on the weekends. I work every Friday night, and at least one shift every Saturday and Sunday. That's when I have the best chance to make money.

"So, don't get mad," Lila says as she looks around the hallway, which means she's going to say something I don't want to hear. "My mom went through her closet and has some really cute tops you might want. You're too tiny for her pants, but she has this awesome cashmere sweater I'd be clawing at if these guys wouldn't burst a seam." She gestures at her chest to make a joke because she knows how uncomfortable I feel when she offers me clothes. I already have her mom's old cell phone and am on their family plan at her parents' insistence. While Lila reasoned she needed to be able to reach her best friend, her mother had a more concrete argument that I needed one for safety since I live in a pretty isolated area.

I used to protest. Eventually, as much as it hurt my pride, I started to accept hand-me-down clothes and electronics. If I don't have work, I'm usually invited to someone's for dinner.

My friends are fiercely protective of me and there's no way I could survive this whole ordeal if it wasn't for them.

"Thanks," I say with measured enthusiasm. I want to appear grateful, but not super desperate, so Lila won't feel pressure to keep giving me things. "I really appreciate it."

"I know you do. That's what friends are for." She puts her arm around me as we go to her locker. "Now let's talk about what you can do for Valentine's Day. I need to live vicariously through you, unless you can find a way to get Conor to go on a double date."

I laugh, but quickly put my hand over my mouth. It's become an automatic reflex to cover my mouth when I laugh, and to smile with my lips closed. I was in the process of getting braces when everything happened. So when the orthodontist bills could no longer be paid, the braces had to come off. My teeth shifted so much in the aftermath that I've developed a gap between my two front teeth. My teeth are worse now than they were before I got braces.

"I was thinking of inviting myself to one of his Dungeons & Dragons nights," Lila sighs. "There'd be no way he could resist my elf mage."

"Ah, now I see the real reason you want to go Cleveland." I wink playfully at her.

"I don't care that he's a huge nerd," she says, cheeks warming.

"Hey, you know I also happen to be a proud and true Nerd Lover."

Brady isn't your typical heartthrob. He's tall and gangly, he's stepped on my feet so often they've become slightly numb, and he wears thick black glasses. But he's sweet and dependable. To the outside world, he probably seems like Clark Kent, but to me he's Superman.

It doesn't surprise me that Lila has a crush on Conor. While he's one of those guys who revels in geek culture, it works on him. He's one of the few kids in our class who isn't white, and he wears his Filipino heritage with the same pride as his Tolkien knowledge. It's rather cool to be around someone so at ease with his geekdom at seventeen.

"I'll put a good word in for you," I promise with a wink.

"If this works out, I so owe you." She starts fiddling with her hair.

"Of course it will. You know, Parker makes an excellent name for a firstborn girl or boy." I bump her on the hip as we make our way to English literature class.

We both laugh as we walk into the room. To anybody looking at us, we're two normal teenage girlfriends.

I have such a debt to all my friends. But at the end of the day, I feel as if I owe much more to myself. There really is only one person who can save me.

And that person is me.

You know that saying, "You don't know what you've got till it's gone"?

Well, I feel like that every time I'm around a mom.

My mother was never like Hope's mom. She made it known to Hayley and me that she considered us nuisances. We grew to believe she'd only had kids because she'd felt she was supposed to. Small-town people had kids, or so went her logic. We were peddled around when we were younger to work events, treated more like accessories than people.

So it really shouldn't have come as a surprise she bailed when things got rough.

I thought our borderline-contemptuous relationship was normal until middle school, when I started seeing how my friends were treated by *their* parents. That was also the time I began spending more and more time at other people's houses. I became accustomed to having second, third, even fourth "homes," courtesy of my friends and, now, my boyfriend.

"Need anything?" Brady's mom asks me as I stretch out on the floor of Brady's room after school with my books.

"I'm okay. Thanks, Helen." Brady's mom is practically my mom, so I don't mind calling her by her first name. She insists more than Hope's mom, and I feel like part of the family. "Well, you know where everything is. Dinner's in an hour."

"Need help?" I offer, although she never takes me up on it. Brady once told me she thinks I work too much, so she wants me to feel as if their house is a vacation for me.

It's more than a vacation. It's paradise.

"You spending the night tonight?" she asks.

"I think I'm going to head home, but thanks."

She rubs my shoulder before heading back downstairs.

I get it's peculiar to some people that I occasionally spend the night at Brady's, but who is there at home to worry about me? Brady's family even offered for me to stay with them permanently, but no way would the family court have allowed that, even though I sleep in Zach's room, since he's away at college.

Besides, this is practically my home. I feel comfortable here. I don't have to be on guard. I'm allowed to come and go as I please. I have the code to the garage door so I can let myself in, like today when Brady dropped me off before his Rube Goldberg meeting. I even have a bag of clothes here for when I crash. The second I got in today, I took a nice, hot shower. It's funny that a shower longer than five minutes is now a luxury.

On second thought, there isn't anything funny about it at all.

These days, I approach the few things I have control over with an almost manic energy. Primarily my grades. I cross off calculus on my list of things to do, happy to be caught up. I start working ahead in a couple of classes, grateful for the quiet and a chance to study. I'm not the best student in our school—that honor goes to Dan. However, I do whatever I can to get a full scholarship somewhere. Anywhere.

I've been working with our guidance counselor on a list of schools that offer generous financial aid packages for people in my "unique situation," as he calls it. I need to keep my grades as high as possible. I'm taking the SATs for a second time to get an even better score. The only thing I lack is a lot of extracurricular activities, since I always have to work. I used to play flute in the marching band, but had to drop out.

I used to do a lot of things.

The one thing I do have is one hell of a topic for my personal essay.

My phone beeps with a text from Brady letting me know they have to work late tonight and he'll miss dinner.

There's a part of me that's growing concerned—not about how much time he's spending working on the machine, but how much time he's spending with Hope.

I can trust Brady, but part of me feels like there's no way I can ever trust Hope.

. . . .

Brady is full of apologies when he finally arrives, close to ten. His dad was about to drop me off at home, but Brady insists on taking me.

"I promise to make it up to you," he says for the second time on the short drive to the outskirts of town, to the River's Edge trailer park.

"You don't have to make up for anything," I tell him. "I know how much the project means to you."

Besides, he doesn't have to be tethered to me at all times.

Then, of course, I'm reminded of how much I need to rely on him. He doesn't have much of a choice, because neither do I. Sometimes I wish for nothing more than to have a normal relationship with my boyfriend, to not have to depend on him so much.

"I can always get a ride from someone else or stay at Lila's," I offer. Brady has more on his plate with the machine. He doesn't need to always worry about me.

Brady clenches his jaw. "It's not a big deal, Parker."

It shouldn't be, but it is. I don't want to add any more stress to Brady's life, but I know I do.

"I know it's not, so I can ask Lila—"

He interrupts me. "It's fine." He says it with such a final tone in his voice. He then clears his throat and rubs my leg as he turns into the entrance. "Well, we know what's next week."

The abrupt change of subject means that Brady's done talking about my ride schedule. I'm grateful to talk about anything else . . . except Valentine's Day.

"I have to work." I know I'm beginning to sound like a broken record.

"Well, I guess it's a good thing pizza is my favorite food."

I look out at the trailers. I don't want to offend Brady, but it always feels uncomfortable when I have to serve my friends or classmates. I know some of them work at McDonald's or other food places, and it shouldn't be a big deal. But it is. It's another reminder of the caste system and how far I've fallen. What makes it worse is my friends who do know the truth always leave me a huge tip. When it first started happening, I tried to give the money back, but that made it even more uncomfortable. So I gave in. And hated myself for it.

When Brady makes the sharp right turn to our trailer, I feel utter dread at the sight of Hayley's beat-up car out front. If I'd known she wasn't working tonight, I would've stayed at Brady's house.

I'm about to tell Brady to turn around, when the curtain in the living/dining room/my bedroom parts and Hayley peers out.

There's no going back now.

"Good night." I give Brady a quick kiss.

I take the three steps leading up to our front door slowly, dreading what's waiting for me on the other side. These days, Hayley is almost always drunk, angry, or both.

As soon as I see she's not alone, I'm not sure if I should be relieved or not.

"It's my precious baby sis," she slurs, then puts her arm around me. "Parker, this is Thomas."

Thomas looks me up and down, leering the entire time. Even though I'm cloaked in Lila's old winter coat, I fold my arms over my nonexistent chest. He's made himself comfortable on the couch/my bed. He tips his trucker cap at me and stares some more.

A chill goes down my spine that has nothing to do with the frigid temperature inside the trailer.

Thomas reaches into his fleece jacket and pulls out a pack of cigarettes. He puts a cigarette to his lips and scratches his brown stubble before he ignites his lighter.

"Would it be possible not to smoke in here?" I ask, my voice tiny, afraid of Hayley's response.

Thomas pauses, his lighter in midair. Hayley glares at me while I want to cry. My protective, loving older sister has been replaced by this bitter person in front of me. The life in her blue eyes has been dimmed. She wears her blond hair in a constant messy ponytail. Lines that didn't exist fourteen months ago map her face.

"Parker," she says in a scolding tone, "don't be rude to our guest."

Thomas puts his cigarette down. "It's okay. I'll go outside."

"No, you can go to the bedroom. I'm allowed to smoke there."

"Even better," Thomas replies with a laugh. He makes a point of brushing past me as he makes his way to Hayley's tiny bedroom.

Once he's gone, she turns on me. "Happy now?"

She doesn't even wait for a reply before she joins him and closes the bedroom door.

It's the most we've spoken in weeks.

Of course I'm not happy. I'm miserable. *We're* miserable. But there's absolutely nothing either one of us can do about it. I can't let anybody know how bad things have become. If I said something to Brady, his parents would call social services, then Hayley's guardianship of me would most likely be taken away.

Then what would happen to me?

What happened to us wasn't Hayley's fault. But it wasn't mine either.

Problem is, Hayley doesn't see it that way.

Hayley was "that girl": head cheerleader, prom queen, most likely to succeed. While my hair always hung straight, her naturally wavy hair bounced behind her as she happily trotted around school and the football field. She always dated the hottest guy in class, had a ton of friends, and was out almost every night doing this or that. Her weekends were filled with parties.

While Hayley enjoyed high school, she *loved* college at Miami of Ohio. She was in a sorority and had a pretty serious boyfriend. Listening to her speak passionately about her classes and how much fun she had with her sorority sisters made me want to study even harder so I'd get into a good college.

That was over a year ago.

She was twelve credits shy of graduation when my parents' payments to the university stopped. She went from being a carefree college student, to someone forced to move home at twenty-one to be the guardian of her fifteen-year-old sister.

At first we bonded over our shared circumstances. Then the shock turned to anger. We pooled our meager resources and hatched a plan: We'd both get jobs and save enough money to leave town together after my high school graduation. It would give Hayley time to save up for her last semester, while I would focus on getting a scholarship.

We cringed when we looked at the trailer for the first time, but the price was right. We mapped out a budget, splitting the costs of rent and utilities down the middle. We would each fend for our own groceries, which was only fair since I was able to go on the state lunch subsidy program. We both had jobs at restaurants, so we could eat at a discount (or in my case for free, within reason).

Hayley began working two jobs. During the day she was the receptionist at a hair salon downtown, then she'd bartend five evenings a week.

The first few months were a challenge, but we survived.

Then Hayley gave up.

The nights at the bar became later and later. She'd stumble in drunk at three o'clock in the morning and kept missing her shift at the salon. I tried to get her up before I left for school, but she stopped even acknowledging my efforts. It wasn't long before she lost that job. Instead of getting a new one, she decided to stick to bartending. It covered her portion of our expenses. Saving for the future went by the wayside.

She stopped talking about college. She stopped talking about any future beyond this town.

I used to bring up online courses for college credit, but she would make some excuse: It wasn't the same, they still cost money, and (the saddest reason) why even bother?

It got to a point where I stopped trying to reason with her, to try to get her to snap out of her funk. It only angered her when I did.

Now we hardly speak. She's usually asleep when I get up for school, and she's not there when I return from work. I pretty much only sleep in the trailer. It isn't a home. It's a bed. A really crappy one.

Hayley used to be many things, but all that remains is a reminder of what can happen to me if I don't escape. She may have given up, but I have not.

477 DAYS LEFT

There are certain days I'm able to navigate easily. Others take every ounce of strength to get through.

Today is the second kind of day.

I was exhausted all during school, after a restless night's sleep. I always have trouble sleeping whenever Hayley has one of her guests over. A couple of months ago, I woke up to one of her "friends" standing over me. Ever since, I sleep with a fork under my pillow, just in case.

Fortunately, it's Friday. I'm spending the weekend at Lila's house, which is a few blocks away from The Pie Shoppe. I only have one thing to do before I'm free: tutor Hope.

I splash cold water on my face in an attempt to wake

myself up. Brady bought me a soda at lunch, since soda's not covered on the lunch program. What I really need is a giant coffee. But coffee costs money.

As I walk to Hope's locker, I debate asking her if she wants to pick up a cup on our way to her house. I can offer for it to be my treat and get a cheap, plain black coffee, but I have no idea what she would order. I don't think she's the kind of person who has to look at prices, and I'm not about to waste seven dollars getting coffee.

Seven dollars.

It's such a meager amount. It was only two years ago I'd get a twenty from my mother for a night out without even blinking. Still, I don't know how I'm going to get through tutoring without caffeine.

"Hi," I say sheepishly to Hope, who looks around the hallway, as if she's embarrassed to be seen with me. She'd have a real reason to be horrified if she knew the truth.

"Who have you told?" she asks, her hand on her hips.

I shake my head. "Nobody."

"Brady?" she prods, finally saying his name.

"No. It's not my place to tell. Why? Did he say something?" Now I'm looking around the hallway suspiciously, wondering why she's so put out.

"No." She looks at me for a second before she turns her back on me. "Let's go."

I follow her, stifling a yawn. It was hard enough for me to concentrate during class today—I'm not sure how I'm going to be when I have to be the one teaching someone. "Sorry," I say, even though I don't have a reason to apologize. I don't want her to think she's boring me. "I didn't get a lot of sleep last night."

She grinds her teeth as she keeps walking.

I decide to change the subject to the task at hand. "How was class today?" I ask as we get into her car and drive away.

"Fine."

"You know, Hope," I tread carefully, "I was really impressed the other day with how quickly you picked up on the mistakes on the test. I bet if you took it now, you'd do remarkably better."

I try to give her a smile, but her eyes are glued to the road, so I stare out the window as well. A pang of desire hits me as we pass by the coffee shop. Part of me is screaming to ask Hope to stop. If it was one of my friends, it wouldn't be a big deal.

But Hope isn't my friend. She barely tolerates me. However, I need the money, and her parents offered me a hundred-dollar bonus for every exam she scores a B or higher on.

I know it's charity, but I still need to earn it.

We remain silent for the rest of the ride to her house, and once we get inside, Hope excuses herself upstairs for a minute while I start to unpack my things on the dining room table.

I hate to admit I'm a little disappointed Hope's mom isn't here to greet us.

Before I have a chance to decide if I should risk eating the banana in my bag that I saved from lunch, I hear the garage door open. Hope's mom enters a few seconds later.

"Parker! Sweetie, how are you? I'm running so behind today. What can I fix you?" She sets down a bag of groceries and looks at me expectantly.

"You don't have to make anything for me, Mrs.—I mean, Gabriela." I give her the biggest smile I can with my mouth closed. I feel a little guilty since I know she'd make me a steak if I asked.

"Nonsense! You girls have to eat. Do you like hummus?" She takes out a container filled with brown paste.

"Sure," I reply, even though I've never had it before. Beggars can't be choosers. Suddenly, a huge yawn takes over me, and I cover my mouth, trying to hide it.

Mrs. Kaplan puts the container down and focuses on me. "Are you okay? You look a little tired."

Tired is an understatement.

"I'm fine. I had a horrible night's sleep." I rub my eyes, hoping the friction will make them want to stay open.

She puts her hand on my wrist. "How are you doing? Really?" she asks in a quiet voice as she steals a glance at the staircase to ensure it's safe for us to talk.

"I'm okay," I reply, because I don't want Hope to walk in on us having a heart-to-heart. "I *am* a little tired."

She nods slowly. "You know what? I'm feeling a little sluggish today as well. I could use some coffee. Would you like some?"

I want to kiss her. "That would be amazing, thank you."

"It's Friday—we deserve a treat. Let me pop downtown and get us some of those decadent mocha coffee drinks they serve down at the café. Maybe some of their sinful desserts, too. Does that sound good?"

I'm usually in control of my emotions, but there are times when the weight of what happened knocks me on my side.

I can't speak. I only nod as tears burn behind my eyes.

I'm running on fumes. Not only from last night, but from my life. No sixteen-year-old should be this exhausted. It isn't fair.

"Oh, hon." Mrs. Kaplan pulls me in for a hug and it's all too much. The dam I've built finally bursts. Tears start streaming down my face. It's torture being so close to what I crave.

I let Mrs. Kaplan hug me. She brushes my hair and tells me that everything is going to be all right. But is it? How does she know? How can anybody know?

The sound of Hope's footsteps wakes me from my daze. I pull away from Mrs. Kaplan and wipe the tears from my face.

"Why don't you use the powder room, and I'll stall Hope," she says.

I close the door right as Mrs. Kaplan asks Hope what she wants from the coffee shop. Once again, I splash cold water on my face. I take one of the soft hand towels and wipe away any physical evidence of my breakdown.

That was too close. What would've happened if Hope had seen? She would've had questions, wanted answers.

It can never happen again.

I need to toughen up if I'm going to last sixteen more months. Once people know the truth, they start to keep a closer eye on me. Which in theory is great, except Hayley's unraveling, and if she goes down, I'll go down with her.

While there are so many people who are rooting for me, there are others, like Hope, who would be delighted by my demise. She was only one floor away from discovering the truth.

All because of a stupid cup of coffee.

476 DAYS LEFT

I don't wake up until nearly noon.

I always sleep better at Lila's. Her home's quiet, warm, safe.

I stretch out in her bed, relishing in the softness of her sheets. After my day yesterday, I'm impressed I woke up at all. I didn't even stir when Lila got up to go to her away basketball game. As much as I want to stay here all day, I have to go back to work in a couple of hours, so I need to get some more studying done.

Plus, I have a deposit to make.

I reach into my weekend bag and pull out the money belt, which has all my tips and tutoring money, in addition to this week's paycheck from the pizzeria. I pad downstairs on the plush carpeting in my bare feet, greeting Lila's parents, who are reading in the living room.

"Sleeping Beauty awakes!" Mr. Beckett calls out with a laugh when he sees me.

"Sorry," I reply automatically. I feel that all I do to my friends' parents is apologize. Or say thank you.

"Nothing to apologize for," Mrs. Beckett reminds me.

"We're going to do leftovers for lunch in a bit, but if you're hungry now, please help yourself."

"Thanks!" I stand there awkwardly in Lila's old flannel pajamas.

"Parker," Mrs. Beckett says in her usual kind voice, "I feel like it's been forever since we've seen your sister. Please let Hayley know she's invited over for dinner anytime. It would be nice to catch up."

"I will," I lie.

Hayley used to join me at my friends' houses for meals. She even spent a week with me at Lila's after we were kicked out of our old house. But she started showing up less and less. I blamed her work schedule, but it was because of her toxic attitude. She once showed up to Brady's house drunk. Right when I thought things couldn't get worse, she threw up in the back of Brady's car. I spent the rest of the evening scrubbing out his backseat.

She's supposed to be my guardian, but at times I feel as if I have to protect her. She certainly isn't watching out for me.

It's because of Hayley that I asked Mr. Beckett to keep my money in his safe. After she was fired from the salon, she started demanding a portion of my money beyond what we'd already agreed to split. So I started hiding money from her. She doesn't even know I'm tutoring. She has no idea of how much I've saved, and I need to keep that secret safe.

I'd be willing to share more money with my sister if it would go to something useful, like classes. But she's spending money on frivolous things. I often see a new outfit in her closet or a carton of cigarettes, which are expensive. Occasionally our wastebasket overflows with venti to-go coffee cups.

A bank account isn't possible, since Hayley would have to be the cosigner on it. I also can't trust her enough to have the money in our trailer.

"Mr. Beckett, do you think I could—"

He jumps up from his armchair. "Of course!"

We walk into his office. He opens up the wall safe and hands me my locked money bag. "I'll leave you to it." He walks out and leaves me alone.

I take the key that hangs on a silver chain around my neck and open up the bag that contains my salvation. The white envelope is thick with money, although the majority of the bills are tens and twenties, with the occasional fifty-dollar bill from when I swallow my pride and actually go to the bank to cash my checks. I make any excuse to avoid the bank after what my father did.

I sit down on the floor with a calculator and begin adding up my newest total. While I keep seeing the tally grow each week, I'm not sure if it's ever going to be enough.

How much does it cost to start over?

473 DAYS LEFT

Spending Valentine's Day at a pizzeria isn't the most romantic option, but it's our only option.

It's Tuesday night and I have to work because the owner assumes we'll be bustling. He's under the impression that the red-and-white vinyl checkered tablecloths are romantic. We are, not surprisingly, fairly dead, although the delivery orders for his special heart-shaped pizza keep him ensconced in the kitchen.

There are only two tables of people grabbing slices. We aren't the kind of place that takes reservations, but I put a RESERVED sign up on the booth closest to the front counter so when Brady comes in, I'll be able to sit with him when it's slow.

I check the clock and put on some more lip gloss Lila's mom got as a free gift with purchase. There isn't much more I can do to look nice for Brady. I have to wear a red polo T-shirt with The Pie Shoppe logo embroidered on it in white, plus I only have one pair of jeans I wear to work, because no matter how much I wash them, they still smell of grease. My hair has to be up in a ponytail so it doesn't end up in people's food.

So really, it's any other day. I begged Brady not to get me anything, since I can't reciprocate. This morning he simply gave me a kiss when I got into the car. I almost forgot it was Valentine's Day until I walked by the school's office, which was overflowing with flowers, balloons, and stuffed animals. Between every class the hallway was filled with announcements of people who had flowers. I stopped listening for my name by lunch. Then when I went to my locker at the end of the day, I opened it to find a wrapped rectangular box. I couldn't help but be touched by the gesture. I turned around and saw Brady behind me with a bouquet of beautiful red roses.

"Now, I know you said no presents," he said as he took a step forward, "but you deserve a million roses and presents every day."

How could anybody get mad at that?

I grabbed his T-shirt and pulled him in for a kiss, not caring who saw it. "Happy Valentine's Day."

"You're telling me."

The memory brings a smile to my face as I touch the silver bracelet he gave me.

All I can give him is a heart-shaped pizza.

But, if there's one thing I realized over the past year, it's how little material goods mean. Yes, I would love not to have to work and take hand-me-downs, but at the end of the day, the most important thing you can give someone in a relationship—be it as a friend, lover, or family—is yourself. Being there for someone is what really matters. Having someone's trust is more important than having the latest phone.

While I had a string of bad luck and hard times, I'm fortunate enough to have good people in my life, especially Brady.

It's getting close to eight, so I know Brady will arrive shortly. The plan is for him to stay until the end of my shift, and then I'm going to spend the night at his house. I'm too afraid to see who Hayley will bring home tonight.

I check on my two tables, and then peer back into the kitchen.

"Hey, Peter!" I call out to my boss, who's busy tossing dough. "How's my special order?"

"Like all my orders: perfection!" he boasts as he tosses the dough even higher into the air.

"Show-off," I say with a laugh.

Peter opened this pizza place last year, when he returned home from college. He'd gone to DePaul University in Chicago, but realized big-city living wasn't for him. He shocked everybody when he decided to come back to his small hometown and open up a pizza shop on the three-block strip that constitutes our downtown.

Peter goes to the brick oven to move around some pizzas. "Ah, here it is."

He proudly sets down the pizza he's made for Brady and me: a heart-shaped pizza, half with pepperoni and sausage, the other half covered with veggies. His eyes flicker behind me. "Well, would you look at that? Prince Charming is right on time."

A huge smile spreads on my face, crooked teeth and all, since Brady thinks my tooth gap is sexy. Although I think he's overly generous.

I take a towel to protect my arms, since I learned from a mistake my first week and have the scars on my inner forearms as proof. I turn around in a fluid motion with the pizza, excited to share this with Brady. But as soon as I see him, I feel like I'm in a horror movie instead of a rom-com. I quickly press my lips together. The plan was for Brady and me to eat together. Alone. It's Valentine's Day. I didn't think it was necessary to clarify the *alone* part.

But there she is.

"Hey, babe," Brady says. But he knows there's something wrong. He glances over at Hope. "We had some more work to do on the machine and I thought she and I could grab a quick bite while you were still working."

"Of course," I reply hoarsely.

Hope looks pretty pleased with herself, as if this is part of some plan she concocted to get to spend Valentine's Day with Brady.

I wouldn't put it past her.

"Is this for us?" he asks when he sees the RESERVED sign with the heart around it.

I nod. It is for *us*. *Us* being him and me, not him and Hope.

They sit down while I stand there holding a heavy and rather scalding heart-shaped pizza. The other tables are getting ready to leave. There isn't anywhere else I can put the pizza except in front of them.

Brady shifts uncomfortably in his seat as I place the pie down.

"I'd already put this order in for us," I tell him.

He looks up at me and I can see the guilt on his face. "This is so great, babe. I'm so sorry . . ." He lets the apology linger in the air. He glances over at Hope, but she's too busy helping herself to a slice.

"Oh, I love veggie pizza," Hope coos with more enthusiasm than I've ever seen from her. "Can we get some plates? And silverware? And I'd love a Cherry Coke. Thanks."

I stand there stunned. Not only is she eating my pizza, she's ordering me around.

I know one thing for certain: This meal is no longer on the house.

"Right away," I reply in my best waitress voice. I turn to Brady. "And what can I get you, *sir*?" My voice betrays me and cracks at the end.

"Parker . . ." Brady tries to grab my hand, but I pull away and instead get my notepad out from my apron.

"We also have a special on fried oysters today." I'm scribbling nonsense in my notebook. I don't want Hope to see how much this has upset me.

Part of me feels stupid. I have to work. Brady has to finish his project, and also needs to eat. But why is it only Hope? If Conor and Dan were here, it would be different.

I can feel a breakdown coming. "Let me grab Hope's Cherry Coke, and I'll be back to get the rest of your order."

I turn around quickly and head toward the kitchen, even though the soda dispenser is behind the counter. I need some space to breathe, to tell myself I'm being silly.

Peter is there, his usual smile replaced with a scowl. "Why is that Kaplan girl here with Brady? On Valentine's Day?"

"They have a project . . ." My voice gives out. I feel tears cascading down my face. It seems as if all I've been doing lately is crying.

"Do you want me to tell her to leave?" he asks.

I shake my head. I want *Brady* to tell her to leave.

Peter's attention goes to behind the counter, while I push myself against the wall so nobody can see me. Peter asks, "What can I do to help you, Brady?"

Brady's voice is measured. "I was hoping I could talk to Parker."

"She's in the middle of something. I'll have her out to you as soon as she can. Is there a message you'd like me to deliver?" Peter loves chatting up customers and is generally a jovial guy, so Brady can tell he's annoyed.

There's a pause. I find myself wishing Brady's going to say Hope is leaving. Or he wants to apologize to me. Something, anything to make up for what he's done.

"It's okay," Brady replies with a sigh.

Really? Because nothing seems okay to me.

Peter approaches me and places his hand on my shoulder. "Tell me what I can do."

"I'm fine," I lie. I go back to the employee room for a couple of minutes to get my composure back.

This is just any other day. Brady made a horrible error in judgment. His competition is less than three weeks away. They have things to do. I have to work. Hope will leave after they eat, then he and I can be alone.

As I return to the dining area, I imagine a few scenarios: Brady will be by himself; Brady will look miserable, knowing he screwed up; or Brady will be waiting for me at the counter with a heartfelt apology.

Instead, Brady and Hope are laughing over our pizza. They look like a couple having a blast. There's no remorse, no awareness of how wrong this all is.

I feel utterly helpless and alone.

Hope

18 DAYS AWAY

I hate Valentine's Day.

I know, what a surprise that a perpetually single girl pining over someone with a girlfriend hates Valentine's Day. Yep, total shocker.

But it's more than that.

Every Valentine's Day starts out the same: My parents canoodle (and that's the polite way of describing it) over breakfast as they sip champagne and feed each other strawberries. I feel like a third wheel in my own family.

Then I get to school.

There I have to suffer through the day where happy couples hold hands and make out in the hallways, reminding all of us unboyfriended and ungirlfriended souls that today is not for us. In between classes, I hear every student's name get called to the office except mine.

I think I speak for every unattached person out there when I say we don't need a reminder that we're single.

As I watch what seems like everybody in high school collecting their flowers, balloons, and teddy bears, I can't help but think: *Why not me?*

Why can't I find somebody who will love me back? Will I ever find that person? All I want is to feel like I really belong with someone.

But then I look in the mirror and the answers come screaming in my head: *I'm not pretty enough, skinny enough, smart enough.*

While I basically feel like that every day, Valentine's Day always stings the most.

So everything is going exactly like it does every year until second to last period, when my name is called. I walk into the office assuming I've misheard the name or that the principal needs to speak with me. Only I *did* hear correctly. There is a huge vase filled with two dozen gorgeous red roses waiting for me.

From my parents.

Which almost makes it worse.

Since I can't fit the roses into my locker, I have to spend the last two periods answering everybody's questions about them. It's as if my classmates can't believe someone would send *me* flowers. Then when I have to admit they're from my mom and dad, I pretend not to notice their looks of pity.

I try to hide the bouquet behind my back when Parker comes up to me between classes. At first I considered making up a boyfriend, but know I'd be caught in a lie she'd never believe. So I'm forced to tell her the truth.

"Your parents are so sweet," Parker replies. "That's really nice of them."

Oh yeah, *how nice* that *my parents* sent me something. I've seen the bouquet that Brady's been hauling around for her. It should have its own zip code.

I've never been so glad to get home, especially since I don't have to be tutored today.

"Who's the secret admirer?" Dan asks when he arrives for our meeting.

"My parents," I say for what feels like the four hundredth time in less than three hours. "Conor's already downstairs. Help yourself to whatever's in the fridge." I take the roses upstairs to my bedroom, out of sight so I don't have to endure the same humiliation with Brady.

Another Valentine's Day tradition is that my parents always spend the night at some romantic bed-and-breakfast thirty minutes away. This is the first year they aren't forcing a babysitter on me.

So I have the house to myself. And what am I doing? Hosting a Rube Goldberg club meeting.

There are nuns who have better romantic prospects than me.

The doorbell rings and I let Brady in. I'm painfully aware he's only here because Parker has to work.

"Happy Valentine's Day, Hope," he greets me.

There's absolutely nothing happy about this day.

When we arrive to the basement, Dan and Conor are

already at work. Conor is sitting in a corner, gluing a ramp to the machine while Dan is working on adjusting the angle of the fan so the boat can cross our fake moat to hopefully hit the target on the other side.

I sit down next to Dan and begin to tinker with the boat that's going to set sail. We're all so busy with each of our tasks, I don't realize how late it's getting until my stomach starts to grumble.

"Hey," I say, "I've got money to order pizza if anybody wants to join me." Mom left a fifty-dollar bill on the counter so I could get dinner. It's become my Valentine's Day tradition: order pizza and stuff my face while I watch some cheesy romantic comedy where the girl gets the guy. Madelyn usually joins me (and groans at the predictability), but has to babysit. Like the local florists, tonight she charges double.

Dan stands up. "I need to get home to study for tomorrow's history exam. So I'll be spending my Valentine's evening with multiple dates . . . of key moments in the Allied invasion during World War II."

"I should probably go," Conor replies as he puts the finishing touches on the ramp. "My parents are having an *actual* date, so I've got to babysit my sister."

Everybody has somewhere to be but me.

I can't bring myself to look at Brady. I know he has plans with Parker. I saw them leaving school today, Parker with her arms filled with those roses. He doesn't say anything as Dan and Conor leave.

The room is quiet as we both continue to work.

"You know." He finally breaks the silence. "I'm heading over to The Pie Shoppe to hang with Parker while she works. You can come if you want to pick up a pizza or whatever."

"That's okay," I reply. How can he be so oblivious to the fact that watching him and Parker on Valentine's Day is the last thing I want to do?

(Oh, that's right, because I've kept my feelings for him a secret.)

"I'll order in." I wish I hadn't said anything about pizza.

Brady stands up and reaches down to me. "Come on, Hope. Join me for some pizza. Parker will be running around working. You're not going to let me eat an entire pizza by myself, are you?"

I can't help but smile. Brady wants me to be there. He wants to spend tonight with me. He's asking me to help him eat a pizza. How can I turn that down?

"Okay," I say as I take his hand and get up from the floor.

He places his arm around me as we head upstairs. "Plus, nobody should be alone on Valentine's Day."

So it's a pity date, minus the date part.

Still, I'm going to take whatever I can get.

We drive separately to The Pie Shoppe, but since downtown isn't buzzing, we get parking spots next to each other. We walk into the restaurant and it's pretty dead. There are only two tables with customers.

Maybe this is a bad idea. I thought it was going to be busy and I'd be keeping Brady company while Parker worked.

(Okay, part of me is slightly happy about the thought of

spending time with Brady in front of Parker. I know that makes me a horrible person, but I have to witness them together all the time. Let's see how she likes it.)

There's a handmade sign at the front booth with the word *reserved* and hearts all over it. It has to be for Brady. We haven't seen Parker yet. Maybe it's not too late for me to leave?

Parker comes out of the kitchen, her back to us, as she carries a pizza. She turns around and it's the first time I see a genuine smile on her face, until she sees me. Her face completely falls when she realizes I'm there.

It doesn't make me feel as giddy as I thought. Actually, I kind of feel crappy about it.

"Hey, babe," Brady says to her. He looks over at me and I can tell he realizes his mistake. Right as I'm about to say that I'm there to place a takeout order, Brady continues, "We had some more work to do on the machine and I thought she and I could grab a quick bite while you were still working."

I'm grateful to Brady for not telling Parker the truth: I have nothing better to do.

"Of course," she says, her voice really quiet.

"Is this for us?" Brady asks Parker as he slides into the booth and motions for me to join him.

Parker looks down at the pizza in her hand and around the room. After what seems like an eternity, she places the pizza in front of us.

It's heart shaped.

"I'd already put this order in for us," Parker explains.

This is so awkward. I want to melt into the wall or go back in time and stay home. Instead, I decide to look down and help myself to a slice of pizza. The sooner I eat, the sooner I can get out of here.

I hear Brady apologize to Parker, while I try to act as if this is totally normal.

Isn't this what I always wanted? To come between Brady and Parker?

But now . . .

I can't handle this silence so I say the first thing that comes to mind. "Oh, I love veggie pizza." I practically scream it through the tension between the three of us. I really should leave. I need to speak to Brady alone. And there's only one way to get Parker to give us a minute. "Can we get some plates? And silverware? And I'd love a Cherry Coke. Thanks."

Parker looks like I've punched her.

"Right away," she says in a robotic voice. She turns to Brady. "And what can I get you, *sir*?"

"Parker . . ." Brady reaches out to her, but she takes out her notebook and starts talking about some appetizer special.

I'm about to stand up to leave when Parker interrupts and says, "Let me grab Hope's Cherry Coke, and I'll be back to get the rest of your order."

What was I thinking?

Although, in my defense, Brady was the one who practically insisted that I come tonight. But *why did I agree?* (Okay, it's because I'll always agree with Brady. He could probably get me to rob a bank if he wanted. I'm that pathetic.)

Parker goes to the back room.

"I should leave," I tell Brady.

"No, it's okay. I wasn't thinking. She's got a lot going on. I'm going to talk to Parker. She'll be fine. She knows we're just friends."

Just friends. Those two words sting. While I know it's the truth, it's worse hearing it directly from him.

I really, really should've stayed home.

Brady leaves me. I sit and stare at the pizza . . . then help myself to another slice. I always eat when I'm stressed. Or happy. Or have any sort of emotion.

You're going to have one more slice, drink your Cherry Coke, and then leave Parker a huge tip, I tell myself. *Leave the entire fifty-dollar bill. It's a small price for such a disaster of a meal.*

Brady's back a few seconds later. "Everything okay?" I ask.

"She's busy in the back. I should've asked if it was okay to bring a friend."

That word again.

I get it, Brady.

This is quite possibly the worst Valentine's Day in the history of the world. Okay, there was that one massacre that happened way back, but pretty sure my heart has been ripped apart and that should count for something.

"I'm going to go," I tell him as I start to put my coat on.

"Please don't," he says as he grabs my hand. "I think I'm in big trouble so I really need the moral support."

I look at his hand in mine. We're holding hands. It's Valentine's Day. There's a heart-shaped pizza between us. I should be elated, but I'm not.

None of this is meant for me.

He shakes his head. "Although let's hope we don't have to relive the Meagan Cooper Incident."

A laugh escapes my throat. "Oh God, you always manage to drive the ladies wild. And not in a boy-band way, in the they-legit-want-to-kill-you way."

Back in sixth grade, this new girl in my class had a crush on Brady. She would follow us home from school. It got to the point where I'd have to be his lookout. I'd exit the school first and look around the corner to let him know it was safe. Then we turned it into a silly spy game complete with code names. We kept doing it long after Meagan (code name Philly, due to her moving from Philadelphia as well as her two unfortunate buck teeth) lost interest.

"Do you remember you climbed that tree?" he asks as he picks up a slice.

"And almost broke my arm," I remind him. "You know, now that I think about it, I don't owe you a thing for the pie incident. A cherry-filled face is nothing compared to the fact I *risked my life* for you."

We both begin to relax as we reminisce about all the adventures we created for ourselves on our boring walks home from middle school. I start enjoying myself and even pick up another slice.

Maybe today isn't so bad after all. Whenever I get down on the fact that Brady isn't interested in me as a girlfriend, I'm reminded of the connection we do have. It's more than anything he's ever had before with another person. That makes me special to him. We, in a way, do belong together.

A smile starts to spread on my lips as I realize Valentine's Day isn't really that awful.

Until I spot Parker looking at us from the doorway and the guilt comes back.

17 DAYS AWAY

"He did what?" Madelyn asks at lunch the next day after I explain all the drama from last night. I sent her some texts when I got home, but something as crazy as spending Valentine's Day with Brady in front of Parker needed to be dissected in person.

"I know, it wasn't the best—"

"What a jerk." Madelyn cuts me off. "Seriously. I never got your whole Brady infatuation, but that's because my tastes run a little less nonfat vanilla than yours."

"He didn't know—"

"Are you seriously going to defend him?" Madelyn's eyes narrow as she glances over at Brady. He's sitting at his usual table with his arm around Parker.

"Well, if you'd let me finish a sentence then maybe I could explain." I take a deep breath. "Neither of us knew it would be slow. He hangs out there a lot when she's busy and she spends hours ignoring—"

"*Working,*" Madelyn corrects me. "Parker is busy working, not ignoring her boyfriend who's coming to her workplace."

"Are you taking Parker's side?" I ask. Madelyn has never been a fan of Parker's. Truthfully, she doesn't like most of the people in our class. At this moment in time, I'm not sure how much she likes me.

"No." Madelyn shakes her head. "I'm taking your side."

"It doesn't seem like it." I poke at the pale brown lettuce leaves that are the school cafeteria's excuse for a salad. I should've gotten a sandwich or something else, but I always feel as if I'm being judged in the cafeteria line about what I'm going to eat. Luckily, this is only the second time I haven't had a homemade lunch to bring. Hopefully it'll be the last.

"I wish you were more mad at what Brady pulled," Madelyn says to me. "I mean, have some self-respect, Hope."

"I respect myself," I reply. In response, Madelyn glances at my salad. "What?" I ask. "I can't eat healthy?"

"That's not it—you can eat whatever you want, but you aren't eating that rabbit food because you want to be healthy. You want to be skinny. You want to defend Brady, because it's as if you've been brainwashed to do so. He can do no wrong in your eyes, but if you really thought about it, there's no way you'd want to be with him after you witnessed how he treats his girlfriend on Valentine's Day."

"Let's not blow this out of proportion! It was a simple misunderstanding!"

Now I wish I hadn't said anything to Madelyn.

She leans back in her chair, studying me. "I don't think you understand the point I'm trying to make. Let's pretend we're in Bizarro World, where you have to work for money and are dating Brady."

I try to pretend like that doesn't hurt. I understand how

lucky I am that my parents don't make me work, but she didn't need to make that dig.

She continues, "How would you feel if he brought some random chick to your work on Valentine's Day of all days?"

"First, I'm not some random chick," I argue.

"Which, in a way, makes it worse."

I push away my salad and decide to glare at a scratch on the table surface. All I did was grab some pizza with a friend who asked me to keep him company. I was the one who decided to leave after a half hour, especially since Parker never brought us plates or my Cherry Coke. I got the hint and left.

So Parker won. She always wins.

"Okay, okay," Madelyn relents. "I get you didn't realize she wouldn't be busy, but come on, Hope. You have to admit you knew exactly what you were doing walking into that place with Brady on Valentine's Day. I don't have a problem with you going after what you want, but don't pretend Brady's some saint. It was a crap move, plain and simple."

My jaw clenches. While I can admit Brady didn't think things through, as I look over at Parker and Brady now it doesn't seem like they're in a fight. They look as cozy as ever. What if last night brought them closer together? And ends up putting a wedge between Brady and me?

"You know I can't stand Parker, but humor me and put yourself in her shoes for a second."

What would it be like to be Parker? I could eat whatever I want and be skinny. I'd have Brady as a boyfriend and ace advanced algebra.

Whatever point Madelyn is trying to make, she's doing a poor job if she thinks this isn't making me go back to resenting Parker.

I don't want to argue anymore with my best friend. I don't want to throw a pity party for poor Parker. At the end of the day, she got what she wanted: alone time with Brady.

I grab a potato chip from Madelyn's bag. "Can we change the subject?"

"Absolutely!" Madelyn lights up. "I'd love nothing more than to never speak of Brady again. Can you even imagine what will happen after your competition? We won't even have to talk about Rube Goldberg machines for the rest of the year. However will we pass the time?"

I can't help it, but I find myself glancing over at their table. Parker's eating chicken nuggets, laughing at something. She looks as if she doesn't have a care in the world. I'd love, for only one day, to be in her shoes. To have everything she has.

I'm trying to remember the last really good day I've had. These past few weeks have been filled with nothing but working on a machine that keeps failing us. A brain that keeps failing advanced algebra. Diets that keep failing me. And, most unsettling, arguments with my best friend.

All afternoon, my mind keeps replaying last night and lunch in a loop. I also haven't seen or heard from Brady since I said good-bye to him last night. It's as if he's avoiding me. Or I could be paranoid.

It's the first time I've ever hoped paranoia was the answer.

And to make everything even better, I have a tutoring session with Parker.

I'm packing my bag after class when I can sense someone behind me. I turn around and Parker is standing there with her arms wrapped around a few books.

"Hey! I didn't realize you were already here," I say to her as I shut my locker. Usually she says hi to me when she gets to my locker, but not today.

We start walking and she remains mute. It's not like we're super chummy or anything, but usually she tries to talk to me about something. I'm the one who shuts down the conversations.

Maybe she's trying to give me a taste of my own medicine.

"Ms. Porter said we're having an exam on Friday," I inform her.

She nods.

Hmm. All right, she's mad. I guess I don't entirely blame her. Maybe I should apologize for last night. Even though the person who really needs to apologize to her is Brady, but he probably already did. And now I look like the jerk.

We arrive at my car and I unlock it. We both get in and put on our seat belts. This is usually when I turn on the car and start driving, but something stops me. While I'm looking straight ahead, I can sense Parker's eyes on me, probably wondering what I'm doing.

Like I have any clue.

God, Hope, just do it. You'll feel better and then you both can get on with your lives.

"Okay, Parker." I turn to her and see that she looks so sad, her eyes bloodshot and puffy. "I'm really sorry about last night. I didn't realize . . ."

I stop myself, because Madelyn was right, yet again. Of course I realized what I was doing. Brady invites me somewhere and I jump at the chance. I don't think about anybody but myself.

Wow. I really can be a jerk.

I sigh. "Okay, here's the truth: My mom and dad spend every Valentine's Day evening together. They left me money for a pizza. I'm pretty sure Brady took pity on me because I'm a loser and invited me to join him because he assumed you were going to be slammed at work. I should've left sooner. I'm sorry. This isn't Brady's fault, but mine."

Why am I defending Brady? Especially to her? Why don't I put them in a bedroom with roses and candles? Ugh, that's probably what they did last night after I left.

I can't believe I'm basically bowing down to Parker to make her feel better. Nobody ever does that for me.

Parker gives me a tiny nod. She finally speaks. "Thank you for apologizing. I appreciate it."

I can't tell what she's really thinking. I try, once again, to put myself in her shoes, but all I can imagine her thinking is that my life is sad and I'm a horrible person. And an idiot who needs to be tutored.

I turn the car on and exit the parking lot. I return Parker's silent treatment, but I feel my chin twitch. Maybe the reason I feel so bad is because I can't believe this is how everything's turning out. I had a Plan and it's falling apart.

The machine's a mess. Yet another Valentine's Day has passed by without being asked out. Madelyn's patience with me is dwindling, and now this. Why can't things be in my favor for once?

"I'm going to get a coffee." I turn to hit up the coffee shop near the house. I need a break before I have to endure feeling like an imbecile for the next hour. I want caffeine, I want sugar, I want something, anything that will make me feel better. "You want a drink?" I offer.

"No, thank you," Parker replies coldly as I get out of the car.

When does she ever turn down anything to eat or drink? She inhaled the big frozen mocha drink my mom got her last week in record time and finished off a brownie *and* a cookie.

But she probably doesn't want anything because I'm the one offering.

I slam the car door behind me.

You know what? I tried. I did. I felt bad about last night and apologized. I refuse to grovel to Parker anymore. It was a stupid pizza. She needs to get over it. I don't know why I even bothered.

It's not like she and I are ever going to be friends.

16 DAYS AWAY

My brain hurts.

I spent the last twenty-four hours doing the fourteen

algebra worksheets Parker gave me to prepare for tomorrow's test. Now I'm swatting away the fumes coming from our garage as we spray-paint and decorate the last few pieces for our machine. We haven't been able to test it all the way through since we've been too busy adding new elements.

I pinch the bridge of my nose, hoping the pulsing in my brain will stop.

"Everything okay?" Mom asks as she sticks her head into the garage—then quickly puts her hand over her nose. "Should I bring a fan in?"

"We're okay," I tell her while I walk out to the driveway to get some fresh air.

Conor looks at all the pieces with a nod. "We're almost there."

Are we? At this point the light at the end of the tunnel seems to get farther and farther away.

Dan finishes spray-painting the cardboard, which will go around the back of the contraption that's supposed to look like a castle wall. He pulls the handkerchief down from his nose and mouth. "Okay, we need to let this dry. Probably best to give it a couple days to be safe."

I'm grateful to have some time off. Especially since this means I can go with Madelyn to Chuck's tomorrow night for a concert. I owe her that at the very least.

"So are people free on Saturday to put the final touches together and do a dry run?" I ask.

Brady and Conor exchange a glance. Am I missing something?

Dan nods. "Yeah, I have to work until two, but can do the afternoon."

"Um, I-I-I," Conor stutters as he rubs the back of his head. "Sure, I have something to do later in the afternoon, but I guess we . . ." He keeps looking over at Brady.

Brady laughs. "Yeah, Conor and I have a little double date Saturday night."

"What?" I say before I can stop myself. "With who?"

Conor blushes. "With Lila Beckett. You know, Parker's friend."

Yes, I know Lila. We're not friends, since she's besties with Parker. It seems like these days a line has been drawn in the sand: Team Parker or Team Hope. Although I doubt a duo could really be considered a team, as Team Hope would consist solely of Madelyn and me. Since Brady has hardly talked to me at all today, I already know which team he's playing for.

"Nice one, dude!" Dan fist-bumps Conor.

"Yeah, I'm about to boldly go where no man has gone before," Conor jokes. Or at least I think he's joking. I'm pretty sure Lila's been on dates before.

"It's a movie, relax," Brady teases Conor.

Mom pops her head back into the garage. "How much longer are you guys going to be? Hope has a test to study for."

Brady glances over at me. Does he know about Parker tutoring me? He has to, right? Maybe I should tell him I apologized to Parker so he can stop being so distant around me.

"We're done," Dan tells Mom. "We'll be back on Saturday to finally get this thing to work."

"I'll head out with you," Brady tells Dan as they walk to their cars, both with a quick nod and a good-bye to me.

Conor stays a few more minutes to wipe the paint off his hands.

Maybe it's because I'm exhausted or it's the paint fumes, but I want to cry. Again. I don't begrudge Conor going on a date, but this little group we have is one of the places I can feel like myself. What's going to happen in two weeks when that's over?

"You okay?" Conor asks. "You seem out of it."

"Yeah. I'm a little overwhelmed."

He nods thoughtfully. "I know, but we're almost there."

Everybody keeps saying that, but what if when we finally put all the pieces together the machine doesn't work? What if we're nowhere close to being there? And, most troubling, what's going to happen once we get there?

We're sixteen days away from the competition. Nothing has really changed for me. In fact, I feel like things might be worse.

"I could really use some of your Tolkien wisdom right about now." As much as we all roll our eyes whenever Conor does his quotes, they've become a comfort to me.

Conor puts his arm around me and dramatically swoops his other hand out in front of us. "Faithless is he that says farewell when the road darkens."

I really need to start reading those books because Tolkien was onto something. Am I really going to give up so close to the competition? Quitting would be the easy way out, and what great thing ever happened by someone giving up or taking the easy route?

No, the guys are right: I'm almost there.

15 DAYS AWAY

"Okay, hear me out," Madelyn says as I shut off the car in the parking lot of Chuck's Friday night.

Usually this isn't the best start to the evening. It means she's going to say something to insult me. Or stress me out. Possibly both.

I keep my eyes straight ahead as Madelyn continues, "I think for optimal enjoyment this evening we need to play a little game."

Sure, that seems harmless enough, but it's Madelyn, so . . .

"What kind of game?" I ask, afraid of the answer.

"You need to do whatever I say," she says with confidence. "But this would require you to dislodge the stick that seems to constantly be shoved up your—"

I interrupt her insult with a loud groan and place my head on the steering wheel. As much as I hate how she put it, she's right. I've been so tense lately. My stupid test is done (and I have no idea how I did—I think I knew how to solve all the equations, but I've thought that before with disastrous results). I don't have to worry about the machine until tomorrow. Tonight should be all about having fun. I'm sixteen years old—things shouldn't be this stressful.

Here's the thing with Madelyn: As abrasive as she is, my best interests are always at heart. She wants me to be as confident as her. To be as carefree as her.

While I know all these things, I still hesitate.

"Hope." Madelyn nudges me so I look at her. "I hereby swear that nothing I'll ask of you will embarrass you or make you uncomfortable. My plan is to set the gloriousness that is you free."

I already know what she's going to ask me to do: dance, sing, and have fun.

What a horrible, horrible friend.

Before I can overanalyze it to death, I agree with the slightest nod.

"Yes!" She punches her fist into the air. "Tonight is going to be one for the record books. Let's go in there and make some memories."

As we walk down the stairs to the venue, I try to leave all my worries behind with each step: Brady, Parker, Mom, the machine . . .

Once our hands are stamped, Madelyn grabs my arm and drags me with her to the front of the stage as tonight's opener plays some grunge song.

"Dance!" Madelyn commands me.

I roll my eyes at her as I start swaying to the music. Whenever I have the urge to look around to see if anybody's watching, I close my eyes or focus on the band. Honestly, dancing wouldn't be so bad if we weren't the only ones doing it. The space in front of the stage is empty. There are a few clusters of people around the high-top tables that line the floor. They're all into their own conversations. There's an occasional head bob, but for the most part it's only Madelyn and me.

After nearly an hour, Madelyn ushers me to the bar while the band takes a break.

"Hey!" The bartender from a few weeks back notices us right away. "How are things in Nowheresville going?"

"As bleak as ever," Madelyn replies. "Although things are looking up now. Aren't they, Hope?"

I nod.

"Cherry Coke and Shirley Temple, right?" he asks.

"You're right, my good man." As he turns around to grab cups, Madelyn leans in to me. "See, we're already regulars. While my plan is to get out of Ohio, maybe going to the U wouldn't be so bad?"

All Madelyn has talked about since as long as I can remember is going to college far away. New York City is her dream. She keeps trying to convince me to head out east, but I'm not sure. I have no idea what I want to do after high school. Part of me wants to get far away, to start somewhere new, but there's the other part of me that's too scared of change. Next year is going to be hard enough.

It shouldn't be a surprise that anytime college is mentioned in my house, my mom bursts into tears. She's aware I need to go somewhere, but I don't know how she's going to handle having her full-time job leave. I don't require much of her time now, even though she insists otherwise. I assume she'll volunteer full-time or go work somewhere. Maybe being scared of change runs in the family?

Madelyn pays the tab and hands me my drink. She scans the crowd of about a hundred people scattered around the bar, mostly college kids laughing, telling stories. Everybody looks at home in their own skin. Maybe that'll finally happen to me when I leave home. I can finally be the person I want to be without Mom constantly intervening.

Maybe college is when I'll finally feel like I belong somewhere.

Do I really need to wait a year and a half to find out?

"There!" Madelyn says as she hits me on the shoulder. She tilts her head to the corner where two guys, one tall and gangly, the other the size of a linebacker, are leaning against the wall. "You need to go over there and talk to them."

Crap. I was having such a good time I forgot about the stupid game. Although maybe I was having fun *because* of the game?

"Are you going to join me?" I ask, trying not to appear as desperate as I suddenly feel.

"Nope." Madelyn bumps me on the hip. "Come on, what's the worst that could happen? They don't want to talk to you. Then we know that they're idiots and not worth our time and we move on to our next conquests."

I can't believe she's making me do this, but of course she is. This was part of her plan all along.

"Okay," I say as I let my feet carry me over to the guys.

The tall one looks up from his drink when he sees me approaching and gives me an actual smile. I resist the urge to look behind me to ensure that smile is genuinely for me.

"Hey," I say over the loud music playing on the speakers above us.

"Hey!" he replies.

I hadn't really thought much beyond that, since my experience at flirting with a stranger is nonexistent. When you live in a small town there aren't a lot of opportunities to meet new people. Not like I'd be a huge flirt if I lived smack-dab in the middle of Manhattan.

"You come here a lot?" I ask, then instantly regret it since it's only the cheesiest, most predictable line of all time. "I mean, you like the music?"

The guy nods, his shaggy blond hair bouncing up and down. "Yeah, we've been coming here since freshman year. You? I remember seeing you a couple weeks ago."

He did? He *saw* me? And remembered?

I'm going to make Madelyn in charge of all my life decisions from now on.

"Yeah, we've come a few times." I feel like I'm screaming to be heard.

"Hey, I'm Ken." He lifts his chin at me. "This is Alex."

The big linebacker dude nods at me.

"I'm Hope."

"Cool."

"Cool," I reply because I don't know what else to say.

Madelyn saunters over to save the day.

"Who are our new friends?" Madelyn asks.

I make the introductions and her exchange is pretty much the same. The band returns to the stage and we lean against the wall with the guys and watch the band from the sides.

Standing so close to Ken, I'm overly aware of my body and what I'm doing. I mimic him by bobbing my head to the music. Taking a drink every now and then. He occasionally leans in to tell me he likes a song or goes to class with somebody. I look over at Madelyn, who's talking Alex's ear off. I wish I could hear what she was saying so I'd know what to talk to Ken about. I don't want to ask him about school, since he'll undoubtedly ask me about my school and my minor status will be revealed. Not as if the big UNDER stamps on our hands won't give us away.

"You want a drink?" he asks as he points to my empty cup.

"Cherry Coke, please," I yell back at him.

When he leaves, Madelyn gives me a thumbs-up. I guess this is going well. He hasn't asked me to leave. He's even getting me a drink.

When he returns I thank him and then take a sip and almost spit it out. It has alcohol in it. A lot.

"You said rum and Coke, right?" he asks over a guitar solo.

I don't know what to do so I nod. I've never had an alcoholic drink before. Mom has the talk with me at the beginning of every year about not drinking, and if I do not to drive. She also always gives me huge hugs when I come home, which is partly because she's that loving, but also, I sometimes suspect, to try to smell booze or smoke on me.

I give Madelyn a look and she gestures it's going to be okay so I take another small sip.

It's disgusting. I don't even think there's any Coke in the cup. And I really doubt that Mom would be fine driving an hour to come pick us up.

"My buddy's band is playing in two weeks—you guys should come," Ken says once the opening act finishes.

The headliner is setting up, which means it's almost time for us to go.

"That sounds like a positively rockin' time!" Madelyn replies. "Right, Hope?"

"Yeah!" I say as I stir the drink, hoping he won't realize I haven't taken any more sips from it. Then I realized something. "Did you say two weeks? From today?"

"Yeah, he's killer on the drums. I can totally get you guys on the list."

I look around the half-packed club. I don't think being put on a list will be necessary, although it's the thought that counts. But there's an even bigger problem.

"I can't in two weeks," I reply. I can feel Madelyn's eyes on me.

What did she really expect me to do? Not go to Cleveland so we can hang out with these two strangers?

"Really? Playing hard to get?" Ken leans in so he's only inches from my face. I don't think I've ever been this close to a guy who wasn't my dad or Brady.

"I have this thing."

Yep, that sounds really convincing.

"What thing?" he whispers in my ear.

I know Madelyn said she wasn't going to make me do anything that would make me feel uncomfortable, but that's what I am right now. While it's nice to have a guy's attention, I don't want it when he's pressed up against me and I can smell beer on his breath.

"Have you ever heard of a Rube Goldberg machine?" I ask. Madelyn's eyes are wide. I figure the truth would be the thing to get him to stop his hand that's now traveling down the small of my back. "My team has a machine in a regional competition."

It works. He leans away. "Really? You know how to make those things?" He turns to Alex. "Yo, remember that sick OK Go video we watched with that huge machine? *She* knows how to do that."

"And it's amazing." Madelyn joins in once she realizes they don't think it's lame. "She's the captain of her team and they are totally going to dominate."

"Cool." Ken holds out his cup.

"Cool," I reply as I tap my cup against his and then pretend to take a drink. "I need to use the restroom."

I excuse myself so I can get some distance and also figure out an exit plan. We have to leave in the next twenty minutes so we aren't late. I pour the drink out in the sink. Before I can come up with a way to leave without seeming like a high school loser to the guys and incurring Madelyn's wrath, the door to the bathroom flings open.

"We're leaving!" Madelyn doesn't even wait for me to reply as she drags me behind her up the stairs. Usually, Madelyn is dragging me *to* places, never away.

Something had to have gone wrong.

"What's going on?" I ask once we get into the car. "What happened?"

"Nothing." Madelyn folds her arms defiantly.

"It doesn't seem like nothing."

"Those guys were jerks."

"Were they?" I ask. "What happened after I left?"

Madelyn pauses, which can't be a good thing. She has no problem telling me her truths, but other people's . . .

"What did they say about me?"

That has to be it. She wouldn't care if they said something about her, but Madelyn's always been more protective of me. Mostly because I need protecting. I don't have her bulletproof shield.

"Don't worry about it. Lesson learned: not worthy."

"Did they say I'm fat?"

"No!" Madelyn protests. "Not at all. It's probably a compliment, but I didn't like it."

"Tell me," I say in such a small voice, I almost didn't realize it came from me.

"That Ken guy for some reason thought in his small, pea-size brain that making an extremely crude comment about your, ah, abundant chest would win me over. Disgusting pig."

I look down at my chest. Madelyn convinced me to wear a V-neck shirt that's snug around my chest. My mom wears those all the time, but I opted for one with an empire waist so it would hide my tummy. I button up my cardigan to the top button before turning on the car.

Maybe it's better not to be noticed at all.

I don't believe it. This can't be real.

I walk out of class, staring at the piece of paper in my hand.

My name is called out. I look up to see Parker waving me down the hallway.

"So?" she asks.

My eyes are about to pop out of my head as I turn my advanced algebra test around to show her my score.

"A *B*!" Parker exclaims. Then, to probably both our surprises, she wraps her arms around me. "You did it! That's so great! Congratulations!"

Her body is as bony as I expected, but being so close to Parker, I also notice she smells a bit like smoke. I didn't realize Parker smoked.

So it seems that Pretty Perfect Parker isn't so perfect.

"Thanks," I reply quietly.

Inquisitive eyes are on us in the hallway. Our school's small enough that people know an odd pairing when they see one.

"Let me look." Parker examines my test, nods a few times. "I think you're going to ace the next one." A yawn takes over. "Sorry, I didn't sleep much last night."

I wince. It's no secret she sometimes spends the night at Brady's. Well, maybe it is, but it isn't a secret if you live only a couple of houses away. Okay, and semi-stalk the comings and goings of one of the house members. I don't know Parker's parents at all, but I can't believe Brady's parents allow it. Mom doesn't let me even have guys up in my bedroom during the day. Let alone sleep over.

Not like there are a ton of guys banging down my door, but still.

"I really needed some good news," Parker says over another yawn.

So did I. We got the machine completely finished on Saturday. We went to run through it and there were five places where the machine either stopped or failed to do what it was supposed to do.

Five places.

And the competition's next Saturday.

"Have you told your mom?" Parker asks. She looks genuinely happy for me. It's the first sign of her not being disgusted with me since Valentine's Day.

"Not yet." Since I literally just exited the class.

"She's going to freak!"

I think Parker's more excited for my mom than she is for me that I might not fail class.

But, as much as I hate to admit it, Parker is a huge reason I did so well. Okay, she's the only reason. I decide to toss her an olive branch.

"Why don't we wait until after school to tell her?" Parker's coming over to tutor me, since one B isn't going to save me from failing.

"Really?" Parker gives me a huge smile. It's the first time I've seen her teeth in a really long time. I didn't realize she had a gap between her two front teeth. Of course it works on her. (Of course it does.)

"Yeah."

Mom is going to freak out. Parker should be part of that.

It's all I'm willing to give her.

"Can't wait!" Parker pats me on the back. "Congrats again. You did such a good job."

I really did. I thought passing advanced algebra was hopeless. I simply accepted the fact it wouldn't happen. But with a little hard work, I did it.

Maybe other goals aren't so far out of reach.

And maybe, just maybe, I'm not so stupid, after all.

"So what's the plan?" Parker asks as we get into my car after school. "Do you think she'll remember you were getting your test back today?"

"Um, have you met my mother, Parker?" I tease. "She remembers everything going on in my life, down to the gritty details. She already texted me. I told her I'd tell her when I got home, which means she's going to assume I didn't do well."

Parker rubs her hands together. "That's so good. Way to throw her off the scent."

"It's become a necessary life skill if I want to get through my teen years only semi-scathed."

Parker laughs. "I'm sure."

Okay, this is bizarre. Parker and I are getting along. It's not as if I've forgotten anything about our past and what she represents, but today's been a good day. We've both earned it so I'll wave the white flag.

For today.

We pull into the garage and Parker's giddy with excitement. I have to admit, it's kinda hilarious. I'm used to

Mom fussing over the simplest things, but it's almost as if Parker never gets rewarded, which I doubt. She does everything right. She must get showered with praise constantly. Now I wish I saved this moment with Mom for myself.

But it's too late. The minute we walk into the house, Mom's waiting for us. She's biting her bottom lip so hard, it looks like it's about to be ripped in half. She's wringing her hands and her leg's shaking rapidly. I try not to laugh when I realize the house smells like cookies.

"What happened?" Mom asks, her hand up to her chest, awaiting the bad news.

I want to milk this for a little bit, make Mom sweat (more than she is now). However, Parker is too busy jumping on the balls of her feet.

"Show her!" she says.

So much for building tension. I reach into my school bag to get my exam. It's barely out of my bag before Mom snatches it.

"Oh, Hope, *mija*!" Mom's eyes well up with tears. "I'm so proud of you!"

She gives me a huge hug.

Yep, all this for getting a B. With such low standards, you'd think I'd have much higher self-esteem.

"And you!" Mom reaches her arms out to Parker. "None of this would be possible without you!" She embraces Parker.

They both stand in the kitchen for a few moments with their arms around each other. It's weird, seeing Mom and

Parker so close. And it's a little unsettling how much both of them seem to need this hug.

Ah, hello? She's *my* mom. It's *my* test. It's as if my important role in all this doesn't matter.

Mom pulls away from Parker and wipes the tears on her face. I mean, really? Mom should've been an actress because this display is all a little too dramatic for me. How stupid did she think I was that I couldn't get a B on a math test?

"Now we celebrate!" Mom pulls out the cookies that were warming in the oven. She puts them on the kitchen table and gets out milk.

Parker happily dives into one of the bigger cookies. Does she ever have to worry about calories? But it would be wrong not to celebrate, so I grab a cookie and take a bite.

"This is so good, Mrs. Kaplan." Hope closes her eyes as she finishes her cookie.

"It's Gabriela!" Mom pours us each a glass of milk and puts it on the counter.

I'm having milk and cookies with Parker Jackson after school. What kind of eerie, demented reality is this?

Thing is: It's not that bad. Don't get me wrong, it's not great. It's not as if having Mom's cookies could ever be bad. But still . . .

Mom claps her hands together. "I know what this calls for! A celebratory dinner! Parker, are you working tonight?"

She shakes her head, since she's already on her second cookie. (And yes, I'm totally counting.)

"I'm going to call Hope's dad and we'll go somewhere special, the four of us. How does that sound?"

Parker finishes chewing. "That would be great, thanks."

"Would you like your sister to join us?" Mom offers.

"She has to work."

I've only seen Parker's sister a few times. I don't even know where she works. It's strange. Parker's family is never around much. Like, I don't even know the last time I've seen her parents. I've probably only met them once or twice since she moved here. It's not like I hang out at the bank where her dad works.

Maybe Parker's family doesn't get involved in every aspect of her life. They probably have dinner waiting for her on the table when she gets home, and don't force her to answer a million questions about every single aspect of her day.

Must be nice.

7 DAYS AWAY

So much for feeling smart.

Although in my defense, Dan's also about to reach his breaking point.

"Are you kidding me?" he screams out when the ball lands perfectly on the button to turn on the fan, but nothing happens. The button doesn't press down and the fan remains off. "Someone hold me back or I'm going to destroy this entire thing."

Okay, Dan's officially broken. So is this machine.

We've been able to successfully get three out of the five issues fixed. All we have left is to get the fan to turn on so it can blow the boat across our homemade moat. Everything after that works until we're supposed to pop the balloon. The lance isn't pressing into the balloon hard enough. Two things and one week left.

I know we can fix this. We've been taking each issue step by step, getting closer to our desired result. So, in a way, our team has now turned into a Rube Goldberg machine (especially the part about doing things in the most complicated way).

Brady places his hand on the fan, but accidentally knocks over a set of dominos we had lined up. In his attempt to stop the chain reaction, he bumps one of our funnels, which took us three hours the night before to get in the right position.

"Crap!" Brady yells as he steps away from the machine with his arms up. "Are you even *kidding* me? Can I have *something* go right for once?"

I look at Brady with furrowed brows because of his uncharacteristic tantrum. Plus, things seem to be going just fine for him. He's three months away from graduation and already been accepted to Purdue, his first choice. He's got a perfect girlfriend. This club can't be stressing him out that much.

"Sorry! Sorry!" Brady says as he paces the basement.

"Brady?" I ask. I take a step toward him. He backs away from me.

"Sorry."

Well, that answers everything.

While I'm tempted to take him upstairs to find out what that was all about, we only have a week to figure this out.

There's no time. Besides, anytime I do try to talk to him, I get a shrug or he talks about the club.

Conor and I, apparently the only two left in the room who haven't completely lost their minds, bend down to figure out what's going on with the fan.

Conor presses the On button. "I don't think the ball's heavy enough to move this down."

"But we can't use another ball since everything leading up to this point has been based on this size and weight," I argue.

Dan takes a deep breath from across the room. "I'll remove the button from the fan to see if I can make it work with minimal pressure."

Conor and I exchange a look. I have a feeling that if we let Dan near the machine and one more thing goes wrong, he really will destroy it.

"You know," I begin as I can feel a headache coming on (my own breakdown will not be far behind), "why don't we call it a night. We can fix everything tomorrow when we aren't so exhausted." And angry. And frustrated.

I glance over at the four-foot-by-four-foot piece of plywood that has so many moving elements that if we weren't under so much pressure, I'd be impressed we only have two issues left.

Conor and Dan start to collect their things, while Brady makes his way over to me.

"Sorry about that."

"It's okay—you don't need to apologize," I reply. What I really want to say to him is that you don't need to apologize for that understandable outburst. However, for keeping your distance from me and not sharing anything about what's going on with you, you owe me not only an apology but an explanation.

I study Brady, and it's the first time he's seemed almost like a stranger. Sure, the guy before me is the Brady I've known for forever, wearing his favorite black-and-white striped hoodie, but I really have no idea what's going on inside his head.

One minute he's reminiscing with me and telling me he's going to miss me, the next he can't seem to get enough distance between us. Every time I feel like Brady and I take a step forward (a confession, Valentine's Day dinner), we take forty thousand steps back (his coldness, and, you know, Parker).

But here's the thing: I'm kind of different, too. That conversation with Madelyn about Brady after Valentine's Day left more of an impression on me than it should have. That wasn't cool of him, even if I share some of the blame. Between studying for algebra and getting this ready, I haven't had enough time to obsess over him. It's only in moments like this, when we're together, that I wonder what's happening between us. Not in the future, but now, this moment.

What *is* he thinking?

Conor puts his jacket on. "Hey, guys, we need to talk about which one of us is going to do the presentation."

I hadn't even thought that far ahead. Someone from the team needs to introduce us, explain our machine, and start the chain reaction. I assumed it would be Dan. He's a senior and the one who has been able to fix most of our problems.

"Hope," all three guys say pretty much at the same time.

"What?" I ask, surprised. "Why me?"

Brady laughs. "Um, you're the one who started this. Of course it's going to be you."

"Yeah," Dan says with a nod. "It's pretty obvious."

"Really?"

"You do have a rather high charisma score," Conor adds.

Ah, I'll take that as a compliment since I need all the good scores I can get. Although, I don't know why I'm so surprised the guys want me to do it. This technically is my club, but still . . . I'm really touched they want me to represent the team.

"Really." Brady puts his arm around me. "Look at what you've done, what you started." He gestures at our machine.

And just like that, one simple gesture from Brady makes all my doubt disappear. Not only what's going on (or not) between us, but what this club has accomplished.

I'd been so focused on the little details that aren't working, I don't know if I really ever stood back and looked at it as a whole. Not to brag, but it's hella impressive. We've built our own medieval world with pulleys and levers and it does something. Well, it'll eventually do something. (I hope.)

I lean into Brady. "It really is crazy, but it's something *we've* done."

The four of us have made this insane, cool thing. We're a team.

#

For the first time since I can remember, the voice of doubt in my head that tells me I'm not good enough and fixates constantly on things I can't control is silent.

Maybe this is where I belong. Not as a girlfriend, but with this weird, nerdy group. Making the seemingly impossible actually possible. Maybe that will be enough.

Although can a *maybe* ever be enough?

2 DAYS AWAY

"Come in! Come in!" Mom opens the door to Dan and his mom. "Welcome!"

"I'm surprised your mom didn't dress up as a princess," Madelyn whispers to me as we stand around the living room waiting for everybody to arrive. Mom decided to throw the team a going-away party, and resistance was futile.

"She was planning a theme. You know she loves her some themes. She even did research on medieval cuisine," I say. "But, she wasn't too excited about making food with cabbage, beets, and wild game."

"Thank God," Madelyn replies with her eyes glued to the table of food Mom put together. She assembled a small LEGO castle as the centerpiece and had a couple of knight figurines posed throughout her spread of different dips, cheeses, meats, and veggies.

The doorbell rings again and I know it will be Brady with his family since everybody else is here: Conor with his parents and younger sister, Mr. Sutton, Dan and his mom, my parents, and Madelyn (my plus-one).

"Aye, enter if ye dare!" Dad says to Brady, his parents, and Parker as he opens the door.

"Dad, it's not pirate themed," I remind him.

"Walk the plank, you!" he replies with a hearty laugh.

"Hi," Parker says to the group while Mrs. Lambert hands Mom some cupcakes with domino decorations on top. She gives me a little wave and I return it with a lackluster smile.

Conor gives her a hug. I haven't been able to get any details from him on his date with Lila. Okay, not like I haven't been perusing their profiles to see any relationship updates or pictures. Parker is pretty much nonexistent online. Most of the photos on her page were tagged by Lila or Brady. It's as if posting on social media is below her. I'm surprised she doesn't want to shove her perfect life in everybody's faces.

But after some . . . let's call it research (*stalking* is such a loaded word), it doesn't seem like Lila and Conor are having some great love affair. I wouldn't even know they went on a date except that it was brought up at that one meeting.

Honestly, all the group's talked about for the last couple of weeks is the machine. We had one successful run-through late (and I mean *late*) last night after every element was fixed. I could barely keep my eyes open during class today. Luckily the coffee shop is on my way to school so I got a huge mocha coffee to get me through the morning.

Parker heads over to the food table and helps herself as she piles her plate with cheese and carrots drenched in dip.

I wonder what it's like to feel as if you can take whatever you want when you go over to someone's house. She's always stuffing her face with the food Mom puts out. Tonight is no exception. And let's not forget (because I never will), she helped herself to Brady the first time she came here.

I think this goes without saying: Life's not fair.

Madelyn strides over next to her and starts helping herself. "Hi, Parker."

Parker gives her a tight smile before heading over to the corner where Brady will protect her.

"Was it something I said?" Madelyn asks me with a wink.

I grab a chip with seven-layer dip off her plate. "Not at all. It's not like you're intimidating or anything."

When people see Madelyn in her all-black clothes and I-don't-care-about-any-of-you attitude, they automatically assume she's a bitch. Yes, she's tough. Yes, she tells it like it is, but she's been such a great friend to me the last couple of weeks. It wasn't like she made some grand gesture, but she simply said an encouraging word there, sent a funny late-night text here. Most of all, she understands how much this has taken out of me. That's all I can ask in a friend: to understand what I'm going through.

I almost can't fathom what I'll do with my time once it's all over. Hopefully, we'll have nationals to go to. Although by that point the machine will be finished. I can actually have fun again. Oh, and study algebra and go back on a diet, and it's probably about time I figure out what I'm going to do about college.

Ugh. Now I don't want Saturday to come if that's waiting for me when I get back.

"How are you feeling?" Mr. Sutton asks.

"Okay. I think you're going to like the changes." He's come over a couple of times to advise, but hasn't seen the finished project except in pictures and videos.

"You've done a great job, Hope." He pats me on the back. "I hope you do it again next year. Maybe you'd like to join us," he says to Madelyn.

She snorts. "That's a big ol' negative. I've seen how much it's driving Hope completely nutso. Let me hit you with a hard, painful truth, Mr. Sutton: With all of the talk about nothing but machines for the last few weeks I feel like I already *am* in the group."

Hey, even Madelyn has to admit it's better than constantly talking about Brady. So take that, Bechdel test.

"Attention! Attention!" Mom clinks her glass. "I want to thank all of you for coming tonight. I think I speak on behalf of everybody's parents when I say we're so proud of you for sticking with this project. Getting to go to regionals is a huge accomplishment regardless of the outcome."

"We're going to crush the competition!" Brady boasts from the corner, where his arm is around Parker's waist. It's a sight I'm so used to seeing. They always seem required to touch each other whenever they're together. I once read in some online article that it means they're an insecure couple, although my parents are always touching and there's nothing insecure about them.

But it's seeing Parker so comfortable around Brady that's really bothering me. She's so at ease in her life. It all seems to go her way with little effort, while all I do is struggle. As much as I try to convince myself that maybe I want something else, I can't help how I feel about Brady. Would I seriously put myself through all the agony and pining for someone if I could help it?

Dammit. So much for passing Bechdel.

Again, that's something else for me to deal with when the competition is over.

So it's passing classes, researching colleges, dieting, and either snagging Brady or moving on.

Man, I don't want Saturday to come.

Mostly because I'm going to miss this time with these guys. Although it's not going to end, because we're going to win.

"Let's see this machine you guys have been spending all this time with," Mr. Lambert says while he nudges Brady.

The group goes down to the basement where the machine sits, waiting to either destroy or make us. Everybody else gathers around the machine, while the club stands behind it.

"Hope," Brady whispers in my ear, "time for you to rock this thing."

"Okay!" I clap my hands. "We went with a medieval theme, if you couldn't tell. Our machine's objective is to inflate and pop a balloon. I should mention there's a good chance we may need to make some adjustments or reset something, so please be patient."

My heart's racing and I'm only doing this in front of a small group of family and friends. I was so honored the guys wanted me to present, I didn't think about having to stand there in front of hundreds of strangers while I represented us. I figured I could work on my actual speech with Brady in the car tomorrow.

I take that cursed marble in my hand and place it at the front of the machine.

With more nerves than I anticipated having in front of a relatively friendly audience, I place the marble at the top of the ramp and let go. The marble knocks into our LEGO knight on a horse, who makes his way down a ramp. At the end of the ramp, he hits the first in a line of dominoes that start knocking over in a swiveling line. The last domino hits the mousetrap, which snaps, pulling down on a lever, then releasing a ball from a spoon, which hits a funnel and travels down a corkscrew pipe. The ball knocks over a water bottle, which dumps its contents out into a funnel. The funnel empties the water into a balloon that begins to fill up. Once the balloon is full, the side of the balloon nudges a mallet, which swings on a string to hit a silver ball that travels down a ramp, hits the edge, drops down to another ramp below, and rolls down three more ramps until it reaches the end. From there, it pushes over a weighted washer with a string attached. As the washer falls, it pulls three evil LEGO knights, who have a damsel in distress in a wagon behind their horses, across a field. The lead evil knight runs into a LEGO cannon, which releases a ball that goes down a ramp and drops directly on a fan's button. The fan begins to blow a sailboat, manned by our heroic knight, across a small pond to the castle. The bow of the ship tips over a glass, which releases a ball onto a tilted xylophone and musical notes ring out before the ball lands on a seesaw. The LEGO knight, on the other side of the seesaw, gets catapulted over the castle walls while the string attached to the seesaw turns on a drill. The drill begins to wrap the string around the bit, pulling another LEGO knight, this one armed with a lance, up above the castle. Once the string is all used up, the knight gets released on another ramp. He goes flying down the ramp, right to the balloon. His spear punctures the balloon and . . . it pops.

It worked.

IT. WORKED.

The basement erupts in applause while Dan, Conor, Brady, and I form a private circle, our arms around one another as we jump up and down celebrating.

"We did it!" Brady embraces me and then kisses me on the cheek. "You're the best, Hope. *The best.*"

My automatic reflex is to look over at Parker to see if she saw the kiss or heard what he said. She did.

Could this moment get any better?

Brady's focus is still on me. It's like we're the only two people in the room. He smiles at me, shaking his head. He hugs me again. "You're amazing. I hope you know that, Hope."

A lump forms in my throat. I open my mouth to say something to him, but I'm at a loss for words.

Dan grabs me by the shoulders. "Did we just do that? Am

I imagining this? Please tell me this isn't a full mental breakdown."

I laugh. "We really did it."

"Holy crap, it's about time!" Conor puts his hand in the middle of our tight circle while the rest of us follow his lead. "One, two, three, Team Knights in Shining Armor!"

"And our fair princess," Brady adds with a wink.

The four of us raise our hands up in a cheer, before continuing to high-five and embrace one another. Tears, happy tears, stream down my face as words of encouragement and congratulations swirl around us from our proud families.

This is my team. All that work paid off. We're ready.

Forget what I said about not wanting Saturday to be here. If I can handle rebuilding a machine in less than a month, I can handle some silly exams, delicious complex carbs, meddlesome girlfriends, and anything else that wants to come my way.

Bring it on.

1 DAY AWAY

There are many reasons to have Madelyn as a best friend. But at this moment, I'm grateful because she knows how to put together the perfect road-trip mix to impress the guy you've been in love with for as long as you can remember.

"This song is insane," Brady says, turning up the volume as some band I'd never heard of until yesterday fills the car while we make our way to Cleveland, with Mr. Sutton and the guys not far behind in a separate car. He insisted on riding with me, so I have taken that as a huge sign that this weekend will be amazing. "You always have the coolest taste in music."

I decide not to correct him that it's Madelyn's.

He reclines his seat a bit, making sure not to hit the machine, which has been carefully packed in the back. "It's good to get away, you know?"

I quickly glance at him. His eyes are closed, a slight smile on his face. He seems at peace and happy.

My eyes return to the road while I try to get what he's saying. Yeah, it's good to get away from school and my parents, but it's not like we're going on vacation. Tomorrow's going to be insanely intense. It's also going to be stressful when we get to the venue later to put the machine together and do a run-through. Basically, the next twenty-four will be mega-pressure.

So I have to ask the question (I really do): What or who is Brady excited to get away from?

"Everything okay?" I fish for a clue. All I've been doing for the last few weeks is reeling out that question to him, hoping for a bite, or any insight into what's going on with him. Truly going on. It can't simply be this competition that's getting to him. Or maybe it's just me hoping there's something else stressful in his life. And that it begins with *P* and ends in *arker*.

He sighs. "Yeah, I guess. I'm letting stupid stuff wear me down."

I nod as if I have any idea what he's talking about, hoping he'll continue talking. But he remains silent, his face leaning toward the sun.

"Do you want to talk about it?" I ask, because maybe he does. He's the one who brought it up.

"Remember the summer before I started high school?"

"Of course I do." That was back when we were inseparable. We spent every day together. We'd either bike to the lake or the park. Or we'd hang out at my house, watch movies, play video games, eat my mom's food.

"I wish things were like back then." His voice sounds sad.

"Do you want to stop to get a coffee?" I offer. We still have thirty miles before I have to exit the highway, but I want to concentrate on Brady right now, not the road.

"Naw, let's get there."

"Okay, but for the record, I wish things were like that, too."

"We had so much fun together, Hope. I don't know . . ." He lets that thought linger in the air.

"You don't know what?" I press. Is it because it's his senior year that's he's becoming sentimental?

"I sometimes wish things were different."

My stomach drops. I want to read into what he's saying. I want to believe he's talking about me. Because I want things to be different, too. I want things to be like they were before her.

Okay, put all my delusions aside. And yes, there are a lot of them. Let's be real for a second: What else could he mean? WHAT ELSE?

"What do you wish was different?" I ask with a slight quiver in my voice.

"Where to start?" He shakes his head before closing his eyes. "I'm gonna try to take a quick nap before we get there. You okay?"

"Sure," I say.

Even though I have no idea how I am or what to think.

Somehow, despite all the thoughts bouncing around in my head, I am able to not only get us to Cleveland in one piece, but get the machine assembled and working in record time.

Brady acts as if nothing happened in the car. He's his old chatting and teasing self as we finish setting up the machine and go to dinner with the rest of the team. I'm fairly positive that conversation in the car wasn't all in my mind. I wouldn't put it past me to have my Brady fantasies go into overdrive with the competition tomorrow, but I know he said those things.

Too bad I have no idea what any of it means.

I go back to my room and lie down. The TV's on, but I'm not paying any attention to it, just like it felt as if I was a million miles away when Mom called to tell me that she and Dad would be in Cleveland by nine tomorrow morning. I'm too busy staring at the ceiling wondering if everything I've dreamed about for years is actually going to come true. Is this going to be the weekend when things start working out for me?

There's a knock on my door and my heart skips a beat.

I've never been in a hotel room by myself. As much as I was looking forward to it, it kind of freaks me out, even though Mr. Sutton is right next door. (The guys are on the other side of him.)

I approach the door cautiously. I don't think this is one of the fancy hotels where they have turndown service. As I glance through the peephole, my throat tightens when I see it's Brady.

I unlatch the chain and unlock the bolt. "Hey," I attempt to say in a casual voice, but know I've failed miserably.

"Hey, thought I'd check to see how you're doing."

"Come in." I open the door to let him in.

Brady is in my hotel room. Just the two of us. He sits on my bed.

Let me state that again in case it's lost on anyone: Brady Lambert is on my bed. By his own volition.

"I was hanging out with the guys and realized I owed you an apology for how I've been lately," he says.

I sit down next to him *on the bed.* "You don't have to apologize. I mean, it's pretty obvious that things have been a bit . . . off with you. I'm sorry if this competition is stressing you out."

"It's not the club at all," he assures me. "It's been a nice distraction."

Okay, but a distraction from what? What happened to the Brady who used to tell me everything?

Oh, right, *her.*

He needs to remember who he's talking to. "You know you can talk to me about anything. At least, you used to."

He looks down at his hands in his lap. "I know, but . . ."

I hate the word *but*. It's always an excuse for something (and I've used it enough to know). That's all I feel like I'm hearing from Brady: I want to tell you, *but* I can't (because of Parker). I want to be with you, *but* . . . Parker.

I'm starting to think it's just his way of not coming out and telling me how he really feels. Maybe he likes torturing me? Maybe he doesn't want to let me go? Maybe he doesn't even know he has me to begin with?

"Brady." I put my hand on top of his. "This is me, Hope. We've been through so much together. There isn't anything you can't tell me. I know you'd feel better if you just got it off your chest."

He considers me for a moment. "I know, I know, but . . ."

Ugh, enough buts *already. Spit it out!*

"I want to tell you everything, but it's not really my secret to tell."

So that's it. There's a secret he's hiding, but it's not his secret. It has to be Parker, right? Everything is always about Parker.

Brady and I have so much of a shared history, it's weird to have something this big between us that we can't seem to talk about. *But* . . .

I'm so sick of whatever's going on with Parker getting in my way. I need to figure it out so we can move on. Once I know that, Brady will really open up. No more secrets between us.

I keep my face neutral. Brady is a talker, or at least he used to be. I simply need to get him to think I already know what he's talking about. I'll manipulate him, just like we do with the machines.

"You mean Parker's secret?" I ask nonchalantly, like I'm talking about the weather.

Brady's head snaps up so he's looking me in the eyes. "Wait a second, you know?"

"Of course." I nod, all the while reminding myself to keep everything about my appearance neutral. I don't want him to think I'm judging Parker, whatever her secret is. Even though my mind is reeling with the possibilities: that she's failing a class, that she cheated on him, that she's a smoker (although I already know that), or, oh God, please don't let it be that she's pregnant.

A realization hits Brady. "That makes sense, with your mom and all."

Remain calm!!! I scream inside my head while I'm trying to figure out what my mom has to do with any of this. How she could know something about Parker and keep it a secret from me. She always told me we didn't keep secrets. Guess I was wrong.

"Is everything okay with Parker?" I ask, focusing the attention back to the matter at hand.

Brady sighs and falls back on the bed. "Oh God, it's a disaster. I mean, she tries to keep it all together, but how could she not be pissed, right? I'm pissed. But then again, I'm still here helping her pick up the pieces. Which actually makes me super pissed."

"Right," I reply, trying to figure out what this all means. It's like one of those equations Parker makes me do, but I need all the factors before I can add everything together. So far I only have x. "That must be hard."

"Right? What kind of parent just abandons their kids? And like, I can tell things aren't good with Hayley. Parker never even lets me inside the trailer anymore. Not like I enjoyed being inside of it, it's so depressing. Have you been?"

I mumble some kind of sound as I try to understand what Brady's telling me. One of Parker's parents has left? It couldn't be both, though. When was the last time I saw one of her parents?

I have absolutely no idea.

None.

But why? Who would do that to their kid? Now I find myself angry at the situation as well. And she lives in a trailer? Did I even know where Parker lived before? How could that be possible?

And how on earth do I have even more questions now?

Brady continues as if he's been waiting years to get this off his chest. "And like, I can never tell who knows and who we need to be careful around. Nothing is easy, because she's so stubborn about help, which makes it worse. I wish she would understand that we're all happy to give her a ride or have her over for dinner. So yeah, this wasn't how I was picturing my senior year, but whatever, it's not a big deal." He pauses for a minute, then gets up and starts pacing the room. "Do you have any idea how hard it's been? It's like there are so many bad things in her life, so I have to try extra hard to be a good thing. I have to be this perfect boyfriend all the time. I'm afraid to make plans in case she needs something from me. And we're not just talking about a stupid ride. I'm talking about a meal. A lousy meal. How messed up is that? I know I have it easy. I know she's the one who has it hard. But I'm tired, Hope. I'm overwhelmed. This isn't my fault, and it isn't Parker's, yet we're the ones dealing with the mess her crappy parents left behind. Then to top it all off, I make it worse by . . ." He collapses his head into his hands.

Just like that, it all comes together in my head. Each piece of the equation begins to fall into place. Parker's parents have left (which I still don't understand), she lives with her sister in a trailer, she has to work two jobs . . .

Oh my God. That's why she eats so much at lunch. That's why Mom keeps giving her all that food. That's why Mom fusses over her. That's why Parker was beaming at dinner that night we went out to celebrate my grade. She was around a family.

Brady's right: A ride and a meal aren't a big deal *to us.*

It's official: I'm the worst human being in the world.

But how could I have known? Especially if it's been this huge secret.

One that my mom knew.

Brady starts rubbing his palms against his eyes.

Over the course of my sixteen years, I've witnessed Brady Lambert display a ton of emotions: happy, bummed, nervous, excited, embarrassed—you name it. But he's never been like this. He's angry, but not at Parker. At himself. But it's more than that—there's a desperation in him that I've never seen. He's absolutely demolished inside.

"Brady, it's okay," I assure him as he continues to walk around the room, his hands now balled up into fists. "Everything's going to be okay."

All I've done is think about me. For years, oh hell, for my entire life, it's been all about Hope. What I want. What I don't have. I could blame it on being an only child and being spoiled by my parents, but at the end of the day, I need to be accountable for my actions.

Madelyn once urged me to put myself in Parker's shoes, and I couldn't really do it because I didn't know the truth. Now I think about it. About what it must be like not to have family around. To live in a trailer. To have to work two jobs and still do schoolwork.

But I also never thought about Brady's feelings. He's torn up over what Parker's going through. He's berating himself because he doesn't think he's doing enough. He thinks he's making it worse. He's this worked up because he truly loves her. He's protected her, not only her secret, but Parker. That's probably why she spends the night at his house.

I never have to think about such simple things as where my next meal is coming from. But she does.

Poor Parker.

I stop telling Brady everything will be okay, because I have no idea if that's true.

"I can't believe it," I say when I finally find my voice. "I just can't . . ."

He stops abruptly in front of me. A look of panic crosses his face. "You didn't know, did you?"

I can barely breathe. I know Brady, but he also knows

154

me. He can smell the deceit on me. "I-I—" I stammer, trying to come up with something that will make him not hate me.

"Are you even kidding me?" he screams. His face is now changing to a dangerous beet color from anger. Now aimed at me. Which I totally deserve. "You *lied* to me?"

"I didn't . . ." But I did. I get up to try to stop him from walking out of the room. I want him to look me in the eyes and know I didn't mean any harm.

"I can't believe you, Hope. I've always trusted you. But now . . ." He shakes his head as he storms out of my room. I jump when the door slams behind him.

I stand there for a few moments to try to process everything that has transpired. My head hurts. My heart hurts. I fall back on the bed and burst into tears.

What the hell just happened?

2 DAYS AFTER

Fourth place.

After everything we went through and all the changes and challenges we faced, all we managed was fourth place. Sure, there were over twenty entries, but still.

Fourth place.

The club is over. While Conor and I have next year, Dan and Brady are done.

Brady and I are . . . I don't know. He wouldn't look at me during the competition. Every plea and apology went unanswered.

There's no other way to say this, but the drive home absolutely sucked. Not only because we didn't win, but because Brady insisted on driving back with the guys. So my mom decided to ride with me and spent the two-hour drive telling me how proud she was of our machine (that was successful, except for the second run-through, where the fan button didn't work so we had to reset it) and me (who has failed on so many levels).

I know, I know, after finally hearing the truth about Parker I should be even more grateful for such a supportive mother, but it stings that she's kept something so big from me. That she and Parker had this shared secret between them.

It only hits me now that my dad probably knows, too.

I spent yesterday sending multiple texts to Brady, which became more and more desperate as the day went on:

I'm sorry. Mom's making a special batch of cookies just for you.

Please talk to me. You have no idea how bad I feel.

I didn't mean to lie. I wanted you to finally talk to me. Please talk to me.

What can I do to make this up to you? Name it. You know me, Brady. I'd never do anything to hurt you.

Please don't hate me. I hate myself enough for the both of us.

All unanswered.

I've screwed up, big time.

But now that I'm walking into school, he can't ignore me. I don't even know what I want him to say to me. He doesn't owe me any other explanation about Parker's history, but what about our history? Yeah, I made a huge mistake, but why is it always so easy for him to shut me out?

Madelyn is waiting for me at the front door. "Hey! I wanted to give the champion a proper welcome into school." She holds out a brown paper bag from the coffee shop.

"I don't see any champions here," I reply, and open the bag. It contains a chocolate glazed donut, my favorite.

Madelyn tilts her head at me. "Hope, you should be really proud of your machine. It was amazing. You didn't win, but you still placed ahead of almost twenty teams. You have every reason to hold your head high."

I nod slightly at her because I know she's right. I should be happy we did as well in our first regional competition, *but* . . . (And there's that word again. Guilty as charged.)

My dark mood doesn't solely have to do with the machine—it has to do with everything. I didn't come back from Cleveland with only a fourth place showing. I came back with the weight of what I learned.

Madelyn looks around the hallway before she places her hand on my shoulder and leans in. "Are you okay? You haven't been yourself—you hardly said two words to me yesterday." Madelyn greeted me at home when we arrived with a sign that read JUDGES BE STOOPID, which had managed to crack a smile on my face.

"I think I'm a little burned out." It's the only thing I can think to say to her, even though it's partially true. I can't tell her the whole truth. I already betrayed Brady; I can't, in a weird way, also betray Parker. Not like she has any idea that I know.

"Of course you are!" Madelyn replies, as she puts her arm around my back as I walk to my locker. "We're going to do a sloth-and-gluttony-filled weekend. You've earned it. Look at all you've done. You've been working nonstop. You should get some medal for being the hardest working student in this school."

I wince slightly because I now know who really deserves a medal (and so much more).

"You good?" she asks as we reach the point in the hall-way where we have to separate.

"Yeah, I'll be fine. Thanks," I reply with the best smile I can manage as I wave good-bye to Madelyn.

I scan the hallway for Brady, to see if he'll finally accept my apology, although I'm not quite sure I deserve it.

"Hope!" I freeze as I hear Parker call out my name.

I'd been so focused on Brady (what a shock), that it didn't register with me that I would also see Parker today. How can I even look her in the eye after how I've treated her? I shouldn't simply feel bad about my behavior because I know about her circumstances, I should feel bad because she's a human being. Nobody deserves to be treated that coldly (present company included, Brady).

I turn around and focus on her feet. "Hey, Parker."

"Congratulations on fourth place. I know you guys were hoping to win, but that's pretty impressive."

"Thanks." I notice her brown ankle boots are really worn. When was the last time she was able to get new shoes?

"I got a call from work that they need me to come in for the early shift after school. Would you mind if we did our tutoring session tomorrow instead?"

"That's fine." I wonder if there's a way I can get her a new pair of shoes without her being suspicious.

"Is everything okay?" Her voice is soft. I still can't look at her.

"I'm fine," I lie. "A little down after our finish." Which *is* true.

"Oh, okay . . ."

"I gotta get to my locker." I turn on my heel and walk as far away from Parker as possible.

I'm so conflicted. I've resented Parker since the second I met her. It's not like her circumstances change the way I think about her as a person, but I can't help but feel really bad about everything she's been through. There's a part of me that realizes even if I did know the truth, it wouldn't have stopped me from trying to take Brady away from her.

And I hate myself for it.

But it's not like Parker and I can be friends now. We're so different. We don't even hang out in the same circle.

Would I even be a real friend if I were only nice to her out of pity?

I need to see it with my own eyes.

I don't know why, but my mind is having trouble wrapping itself around everything I learned. So I find myself driving at nine o'clock at night to the one trailer park outside of town. I had to look it up online because until Brady mentioned it, I had no idea it even existed. Talk about a life of privilege (and blissful ignorance).

I see the sign for River's Edge, turn into the entrance,

and put my dimmers on so I hopefully won't be recognized. Not like it'll help much. When your dad gets you a shiny new red car for your sixteenth birthday, you sort of stand out.

There are about four rows of trailers. Some are surprisingly big with porches and window boxes filled with flowers.

Maybe it's not so bad.

I turn the corner to find a few that are tiny and look a little worse for wear. Since it's dark, I can see inside the ones that have lights on and their curtains open. I slow the car down as I start looking into each trailer. My foot slams on the brakes when I spot the top of Parker's head in the back of one of the smaller trailers. She has a blanket wrapped around her and a wool hat on. That trailer is white with a blue stripe, but there's rust dotting the entire outside. I see the wood paneling behind her, but nothing else. Her head is down like she's reading something or studying.

Headlights from another car flash in my rearview mirror and I step on the gas and head toward the exit.

I don't know what to think besides the fact that life isn't fair. Not because I don't have a boyfriend or I carry a few extra pounds. *This* is what isn't right with the world.

Parker shouldn't have to live like this.

I always thought I knew what I wanted: a boyfriend, a perfect body, to not have to study so much, for things to come easy for me. But now I think about what I do have: a family, a house, security . . .

Now I have no idea what I want.

Parker

453 DAYS LEFT

Something happened in Cleveland.

I've never been the jealous-girlfriend type, mostly because I've had bigger issues to deal with than dating. However, Brady's been acting strange since he got back from Cleveland. He's quiet and won't look me in the eye. At first I chalked it up to being disappointed in not winning, but I can tell something else is going on.

"I have to work after school," I tell him as he pulls into the parking lot Monday morning.

"Okay," he replies. It's the first word he's spoken in nearly ten minutes.

"I'm going to have Lila take me."

"Okay."

We get out of the car and walk toward school. Usually he wraps his arm around me, but instead his arms are clutching his backpack, his gaze on the ground.

I look around the hallways, wondering if I could find a clue as to why he's being so distant, but I can only come up with one explanation: Hope.

He was with her all weekend. There was a hotel.

Here I thought I could trust Brady. Unfortunately, I've been fooled one too many times with people I've assumed I could trust. Like my parents. And Hayley.

Things with my sister have gotten even worse. There's a new guy she's been bringing home, Evan. His hands always linger around my waist when he insists on hugging me every time he sees me. His lips get a little too close when he whispers in my ear. I've debated bringing it up to Hayley, but I've been in this circumstance before and she accused me of hitting on the guy. I don't need yet another wedge placed between us. There's already too much distance and contempt.

I had to spend five dollars on a fabric refresher because I can't seem to get his cigarette smoke out of my clothes. I'm now going over to Lila's twice a week to do laundry. I keep my clothes tied tightly in a plastic bag, but all it takes is one visit from Evan and everything reeks. Ms. Porter even pulled me aside one day after class to see if I'd started smoking.

At least you can quit smoking. It's harder to quit family. Unless you're my parents.

"I got to talk to Dan," Brady mutters before heading down the hallway. We always walk to class together. Or at least there's a quick kiss or a hug, something to hold on to. I've never been the needy type, but I grasp on to whatever normalcy remains in my life. Piece by piece things have begun to slip away from me, and I fear Brady is next.

I turn down another hallway to get some distance from Brady and my thoughts, when I see Hope walking up ahead.

Before I can think everything through, I call out her name. Things with us have gotten a little bit better. At least she doesn't seem to resent me as much. However, there's something else that's pulling me toward her. I need to see how she'll act around me to confirm if my suspicions are correct.

She turns around, but her gaze remains at the floor. "Hey, Parker."

I look down at the floor as well, trying to figure out why both Brady and Hope seem to find it so interesting as of late. Although there's a sinking feeling in my empty gut that I already know why. Maybe Hope finally got what she's always wanted.

But that can't be it, can it?

Am I so dependent on Brady that I'm willing to turn a blind eye to the growing evidence that something clearly happened between the two of them?

Perhaps it's simply because of their fourth-place finish. As someone who's been struggling to stay above water for so long, I'd be thrilled with fourth place in anything.

"Congratulations on fourth place. I know you guys were hoping to win, but that's pretty impressive." I give her a smile, but she doesn't notice it since her focus is on my feet. Now I feel self-conscious about my ratty boots. I'm lucky my feet have stopped growing so I haven't needed to buy new shoes in a while, but clearly I'm due for a new pair.

"Thanks." Her knee starts shaking as if she's nervous.

"I got a call from work that they need me to come in for the early shift after school. Would you mind if we did our tutoring session tomorrow instead?"

"That's fine."

She doesn't seem mad at me, which is a nice change. She doesn't even come off as guilty about what may or may not have happened. Honestly, if Hope did hook up with Brady, she'd probably dance around the hallways. No, Hope isn't happy. In fact, she seems really sad. "Is everything okay?"

"I'm fine. A little down after our finish."

"Oh, okay." I look around the hallway to make sure nobody can hear me. I'm about to tell her she can talk to me, when she abruptly states she has to get to her locker and leaves.

Maybe it really is the fourth-place finish that has them behaving suspiciously, but I can't shake the feeling it's something else.

And it has to do with me.

I haven't had a lot of good days in the past year.

Most days have been bearable, but that's it. However, I did have one of my favorite days in the last month when Hope got a B on her test. Going home with Hope and seeing her mom's reaction made me ache for a mom. Not my mom, but a mom like that. But instead of being sad, I was actually happy because I felt like part of a family that day.

Hope's mom insisted I go out to dinner with them. Her parents asked me how my day was and seemed interested in me as a person. I wasn't a hindrance to them or a chore.

I was someone they genuinely wanted to know about. They made sure I had plenty to eat and forced leftovers on me. I didn't protest because I could tell they wanted to help me. They cared.

It was touching to have a parent want to take care of me. I'm sixteen. Someone should be taking care of me.

I know so many of my friends talk about how they can't wait to go off to college, to be independent and on their own.

Let me tell you something: Being on your own is overrated. I've been on my own since I was fifteen. It's not fun. It's exhausting.

All I really want is a family. I know it's not something that's going to come to me easily, but that night, for a small sliver in time, I felt as if I had one.

I had a smile on my face the entire night. It only went away when I walked into our trailer and had to stop playing pretend and adjust back to my reality.

A shock of cold air greets me in our trailer when Lila drops me off after work.

I go over to the heater to turn it up. We keep the heat either off or on low when we aren't home, to save money, but as I adjust the temperature, nothing comes out. It's always a little frigid in the trailer even with the heater working. I don't want to think about how cold it's going to get tonight. Even though it's early March, it's still pretty chilly outside. I wrap myself up in my sleeping bag and put on my wool hat and a pair of fingerless gloves while I finish up my homework.

Headlights flash into the window and I bundle up tighter waiting for Hayley to come through the door and freak out over the heating situation.

I fight the bile rising in my throat as I hear her key in the door, and wrap myself tighter still when I hear Evan's voice.

Hayley's fake laughter bursts through the door with her. "You're so bad!" She swats Evan's hand off her butt.

"Hey, little one," Evan says with a wink.

I nod and return to my homework. Wishing, praying they'll go back to her room and leave me alone.

"It's freezing in here!" Hayley screams while she runs over to the thermostat.

Evan sits down right next to me. He presses his leg into mine. I've never been so grateful for a sleeping bag as a barrier.

"Why didn't you turn it up?" Hayley asks.

"I think it's broken." I hold my breath, knowing somehow she'll find a way to blame this on me.

She fiddles with the thermostat while cursing under her breath. I continue highlighting the reading selection for English, while ignoring Evan's hot tobacco breath on my neck. "Need help?" he offers. "I used to do good in English."

Yes, so it seems.

"I'm fine," I reply, scooting over a few more inches to get space between us.

He follows me and puts his arm around me. "I've got a great idea for how you can warm up."

"Evan!" Hayley calls out. "Can you look at this stupid thermostat? I need to have a talk with my sweet baby sister."

Of course Hayley isn't upset at Evan for practically sitting on my lap. She, instead, is going to get mad at me for something I can't control. All I hope is that it won't cost too much to get the heater fixed. Evan spends all of three seconds looking at the thermostat before giving up and heading into Hayley's bedroom.

"It wasn't working when I got home," I begin to explain.

"Of course," Hayley says in a surprisingly understanding tone. She sits down next to me and takes my cold hands into hers. "How are you doing? Everything good?"

I'm taken aback by her questions. These are the kind of questions any sister—or, in our case, *guardian*—should ask, but I can't remember the last time she seemed to truly care about what was going on with me.

"Everything's fine," I lie. As much as I'd love to open up to my sister, I don't entirely trust her motives.

"What's new?" She crosses her legs, leaning back into the couch. "How are things with Brady? And work?"

"Good," I reply cautiously. "How are things with you?"

"Great!" Her voice rings false. We both know things aren't great. "Nothing new, then? Something that may have slipped your mind?"

I study Hayley, wondering what she's getting at. We haven't had a real conversation in months. There is a lot I haven't told her, but she hasn't seemed to care.

I shake my head. "I don't think so."

What I really want is to smash the wall that's been built between us. But I don't trust her. It makes me so sad, and frustrated, that I can't trust my own sister, but Hayley isn't the same person she used to be.

Then again, who really is?

Hayley reaches out and tucks a strand of hair behind my ear. I feel a crack in our wall. It's such a tiny gesture, but it's intimate and caring. Something I've been craving from her, or any family member, for nearly a year.

"See, I know you're a lying little bitch." She wraps her hand around a section of my hair and yanks down hard.

I cry out in pain. "What are you doing? Please, Hayley!"

She lets go of my hair and stands up. "I ran into Gabriela Kaplan today at the coffee shop. Imagine my surprise when she started telling me how my sweet baby sister has been tutoring her daughter."

No. It never even occurred to me to tell Mrs. Kaplan that my tutoring is a secret. How could I? I'd have to admit there are problems with Hayley.

Everybody has their secrets, but this is my biggest. Nobody, and I mean not a single soul, has any idea things have gotten this bad. If one person finds out Hayley is unfit to be my guardian, I'll be taken away. While that might appear to be a promising solution to my problems, I have no idea what would happen to me. I'd rather take my chances on the devil I live with.

"I'm sorry," I say in a whimper. "It's not much money. I've been saving it for college."

Hayley's laugh is cruel. "Oh, it's so *precious* you think

you're going to escape. You think you get to have some perfect life while I'm left here to rot? *Think again.*" She holds out her hand. "I want that money. Now."

"I don't have it. I used it to pay for the SAT I'm taking in a couple weeks." This isn't a total lie. I did use some of my tutoring money, but the rest is in the safe at Lila's house, where it belongs.

She reaches into her back pocket and pulls out her phone. "Do I need to call that woman and ask her how much money she's given you? You need to pay your way around here. There aren't any free rides."

My entire body is shaking, and not just from the temperature. I stand up. "I have more than paid my dues. I'm not going to give you a single extra cent to pay for your cigarettes, booze, and overpriced coffees."

"How dare you?" She spits at me. "Do you have any idea how hard I'm working?"

"Do you have any idea how hard *I'm* working? And I also have school. Besides, I haven't given up like you."

The second I say it, I regret it. Hayley's eyes narrow. "You spoiled little brat."

A laugh escapes my throat as I unzip myself from my sleeping bag. "Oh yes, I'm *so* spoiled. I haven't bought a new item of clothing in a year. What about you?" I run over to the closet and start pulling out all of Hayley's new clothes. "Here's twenty-four dollars!" I yell as I throw a scarf that still has its price tag on. I feel as if everything I've been holding in for the last several months releases and it can't come out fast enough.

"And don't even get me started on your coffee habit." I pull out the trash can from under the sink. I start throwing empty cups at her while screaming, "Four, five dollars per cup! *This* is where your money's going. Don't blame it on me."

There's a knock at the front door. "Everything okay in there, girls?"

Hayley and I exchange matching looks filled with panic. I swallow down the rest of my venom and try to calm down while Hayley pushes me out of the way.

She opens up the door to our elderly next-door neighbor. "Hello, Mrs. Richards," Hayley coos. "I'm so sorry if we're being loud—simply a little sisterly argument. We're all made up now. No worries at all. You have a lovely evening."

"Wanted to make sure everything's okay in here," she says as she looks over at me. I can barely produce a smile to convince her my life isn't hanging together by a fraying piece of thread. "We've got to look out for each other."

"Yes, we do," Hayley replies before shutting the door.

That's rather ironic since I can't remember the last time Hayley looked out for anybody but herself. It's why I'm hoarding my hard-earned money to ensure I can get out of here.

But if I don't look out for myself, who will?

"This isn't over," Hayley hisses at me. "Trust me, you're going to pay."

She walks to the back and slams her bedroom door shut.

Haven't I already paid enough?

Maybe this makes me a heartless person, but I always knew Brady and I would eventually break up.

It wasn't as if I was deluding myself into thinking we'd ride off into the sunset and get married. There's been this assumption between us that we'd end things before he left for Purdue in the fall. There was always a possibility it could end sooner, but I never thought it would end because of Hope.

"So what are you going to do?" Lila asks me after school as we're hanging out at her locker. Truthfully, I'm simply stalling before I have to go meet up with Hope and endure yet more of her awkward behavior.

"I've tried to ask him if there's anything wrong and he brushes me off," I reply as I gently rub the part of my head that's still sore from Hayley pulling my hair last night. I sigh. Maybe I should get the inevitable over with. I have too much going on to deal with boy drama. Plus, as scary as it is, I really need to be better standing on my own. It's not fair to Brady that I use him as a security blanket.

Yet there's another part of me that wants to cling to him, since he represents part of my old life, and I want to grasp on to those measly scraps that remain.

Lila shakes her head. "I can't believe he'd cheat on you with *her*."

"Hope's used to getting what she wants," I state before a giant yawn takes over me. Needless to say, I didn't sleep well last night. I never do when Evan's over.

"I don't think you should give up on him yet." Lila links her arm with mine as we walk down the hallway.

"That or you simply want more double dates," I tease her. "Does Conor seem different since Cleveland?"

"Conor's always different, which is why I like him."

I stop when I see Hope at her locker. She looks up from her bag and sees me. She gives a little wave with a forced smile.

"Ew," Lila says under her breath. "Yeah, something's up with her. She looks guilty as hell."

"Off to serve my sentence." I give Lila a hug good-bye, more grateful than ever to have her. It's difficult to deal with Hope on a good day, but I'm too confused and drained today. Since I need the money, I try to put a spring in my step as I walk over to her.

"Hey, Parker!" Hope says with an unusual nervous quiver in her voice. "How was your day?"

"Good," I reply cautiously. She's never asked me about my day before. "How was yours?"

"Can't complain."

That's refreshing. She's usually put out by something or someone, often her mom and most often me.

I cover my mouth as another yawn takes over. "Sorry." I don't know why I constantly feel the need to apologize to people when I yawn. I am sorry, but because this is what I've been reduced to, practically sleepwalking through life.

"It's totally fine." Hope's eyes get wide as if she's suddenly realized something. "You know what I could use?

Some coffee! Yes! Let's go grab coffee on our way to my house. It will totally be my treat, of course! How does that sound?"

It sounds great, but I can't help but think it's some sort of trap. Perhaps Hope is under the impression she can buy my forgiveness with a cup of coffee. I've had so much betrayal in my life, it would take a lot more than some hot water and coffee beans to even begin to make a dent.

"Only if you want," I say.

"I do!"

One thing I've learned is that I should take the good with the bad. So I should be grateful Hope's in a good mood and being generous. However, there's a little voice in my head telling me the only explanation for her unusual behavior is guilt for whatever happened in Cleveland.

The entire ride to get coffee, Hope peppers me with questions about work and school. I politely answer, the entire time feeling my guard strengthen. She's setting me up. For what I don't know, but nothing is ever truly free, especially when Hope's involved.

We walk into the coffee shop and I scan the menu.

"What would you like? Anything! Remember it's on me!"

"I'll take a small black coffee, thanks." While I appreciate the gesture in theory, I don't want her to think buying me one coffee is going to buy my forgiveness for cheating with my boyfriend. Because in reality, what else could have happened in Cleveland between her and Brady?

"What?" Hope shakes her head. "That's so boring! What about the mocha frappé? It's so good!"

It is good, really good, but expensive. I know Hope has the money, but I don't want to take advantage even though I can't help but feel I'm the one who's actually being taken advantage of. I decide to compromise. "Okay, I'll have a small."

"Do you want a brownie? Or a cookie? Again, my treat!"

Yes, I'm aware this is all Hope's treat. She takes a twenty-dollar bill out of her wallet as if it's nothing. Anytime I hold a twenty, I think of all it can buy me. I'd never waste it on coffee and treats. I'm not my sister.

"I'm okay, thanks," I reply as I take a step back while she orders for us. I always feel uncomfortable whenever anybody else picks up the bill. Which is saying a lot since I'm rarely in a situation when I can afford to pay.

"I love this place," Hope says as we wait for our order. "Do you come here a lot?"

"Not really. My sister does." I think about all the coffee cups I threw at her last night.

"That's cool."

We wait in more uncomfortable silence as we pretend to be really interested in whatever the people around us are ordering or picking up.

"Here's your food!" One of the people behind the counter hands Hope a brown paper bag.

"I couldn't resist getting some little treats—it all looked so good." She opens up the bag and hands me a giant brownie. "Here, it's yours!"

"Thanks," I say to her again, more out of habit and

politeness than actual gratitude. I'd usually devour something so decadent, but I've lost my appetite. Hope's trying
to get on my good side before she knocks me down.

She looks down at my battered shoes. "Hey! What size
shoe are you?"

Now she wants to know my shoe size? "Seven and a half."

"Really? I'm an eight and I have this awesome pair of
boots that are too tight on me—maybe they'd be perfect for
you? I've already worn them once so I can't return them.
When we get to my house, I'll have you try them on."

I don't even know how to reply to her random offer. Her
name is called and she's handed our drinks. She gives me a
large mocha frappé. "I figured I should get you the big size.
Enjoy!"

She holds out her latte to toast. I oblige, but then catch
that familiar look in her eye: pity.

The coffee. The treats. The shoes. It's all making sense
to me now.

I look down at my drink. Now I'm the one who can't make
eye contact. My mind races as I try to steady my breath and
not show that I figured it out.

Something did happen in Cleveland.

Hope knows the truth.

It was never supposed to be this big secret.

In a town this small, I assumed everybody would find
out eventually. When everything started happening, the
last thing I worried about was what other people knew.

First, Dad didn't come home from work at the bank. I didn't really notice anything until the next morning, when it was only Mom and me at the kitchen table for breakfast. She was staring into her cup of tea while I made myself some toast. She kept checking her phone, even calling Dad a few times.

"Is everything okay?" I asked her. We were never ones for big heart-to-hearts, but it was clear something was off. "Where's Dad?"

"I don't know," she replied while placing another call.

"What? Is he hurt? Have you called the hospital?" Immediately my mind came up with worst-case scenarios. Why wasn't Mom panicking? "Did you call the police?"

But she didn't call the police, because they were soon at our door. The moment the red and blue lights reflected through the window, Mom started crying.

Dad's dead was my first thought.

Mom was inconsolable as the police started asking her about where Dad was, where the money was, what she knew . . .

I had no idea what was going on. I'd never heard of embezzlement or money laundering. My naïveté didn't stop the police from taking both of us to the police station for questioning. Mom had called our family lawyer that I hadn't even known existed. The lawyer sat next to me while the police started asking me all these questions about Dad's work and if I knew where he'd possibly be.

I knew nothing. I was clueless.

Slowly, it started coming together. He took money that

didn't belong to him. I suspected Mom knew, but she insisted on her innocence. The bank was keeping what happened quiet to not upset its customers, especially since their money was insured. So most people didn't know what was happening to my family.

Two days after Dad left, I woke up to an empty house. I'd assumed Mom was simply out running an errand. She didn't return for the rest of the day. She wasn't answering her phone. I made myself breakfast, then lunch, and then dinner, assuming she'd eventually return.

By the third day, I didn't know what to do or who to call. I was frightened and confused. Nothing that had happened in the last seventy-two hours made any sense. Mom had lied to the school, saying that I had the flu, but without her home, I did the only thing that was normal. I went to school. Lila's parents picked me up. I told them my mom wasn't feeling well.

My life was turning upside down, but as soon as I stepped inside school, everything was the same. Nothing had changed: the hallways, the classrooms, the cafeteria, my teachers and classmates—it was all still there. It was a relief to have the normalcy of classes and homework.

I went home that night to an empty house. I kept trying Mom's phone. My calls immediately went to voice mail. I reached Hayley at college to see if she'd heard from Mom or Dad. She hadn't, but she did talk to the police. She assured me everything was going to be fine. And I believed her, because that was back when I could trust Hayley. Back when she had my back. Or maybe I wanted to believe her because I couldn't fathom the other possibility. The one that would soon be my reality.

I went to school the next day. But by the time I got home, the house wasn't empty. The police were there. They started asking more questions I couldn't answer. My mom had simply vanished.

"Is there somebody I can call?" the sheriff had asked.

I didn't have anybody but Hayley. A social worker came over and talked to me. Finally, Lila's family was brought to my house and filled in on what had happened. I was going to stay with them for a couple of days until my mom came home.

At that time, I had expected Mom would come home. She wouldn't simply abandon her daughter or leave without a good-bye.

That night, when Mrs. Beckett tucked me in, she stroked my face and told me it was all going to be okay. That was the first time I saw that look. The one I've come to despise so much.

I've seen it so much this last year. Two weeks after my mom left, the social worker and sheriff sat me down with my growing support group that consisted of Lila's parents, Brady's parents, and Hope's mom. With that look, they told me that they didn't think my mom was coming back. That whatever assets my parents hadn't taken with them were being seized by the government. It took me a while to realize that meant there was no money and I had no home. There wasn't anything to pay for Hayley's college or even something as insignificant as my braces. They wanted to do a big community fund-raiser, but I begged them not to do it.

School was one of the few places I didn't have to endure that look. The cafeteria workers were aware I was on the school lunch program, a few friends knew, but that was it.

I desperately wanted to keep it a secret so people wouldn't pity me. I didn't want what my parents did to define who I was. I started formulating a plan with Hayley to get out of town. To get away from a past that haunts me, from the people who judge me because of what my parents did, and most of all, to get as far away as possible from that look.

Over time, that look has somewhat faded from those who know the truth. I've become a part of Lila's and Brady's families. Mrs. Kaplan simply wants to make sure I'm fed. Even the lunch ladies seem more impressed by how much I can eat than feel sorry for me anymore. The social worker merely sees me as someone she needs to keep tabs on until I turn eighteen.

There are days, especially at school, when I feel normal again. I'm just another student.

But that's been taken away from me.

451 DAYS LEFT

When I really think about it, it was inevitable.

"We need to talk," I tell Brady when we get into his car after school the next day.

"Okay, but we talk all the time." He winks at me in an attempt to lighten the mood.

Yes, we used to talk all the time. Now, every word and movement between us has been strained. We're like two dancers out of synch. While I would have preferred for Hope not to know my situation, it isn't the end of the world. Or at least, it doesn't need to be.

"I'm not going to be mad, but I need to know. Did you tell Hope about me?"

Brady's forced smile falters. He drops his head. "I'm sorry."

"Is that why you've been so distant lately? I'll admit I'm not thrilled about it, but we can get through this." I didn't need to remind him we've been through worse. "Granted, I could do without her not even remotely subtle attempts to give me things. Still, it's nice she seems to hate me less."

As much as I wish she didn't know, I made the conscious decision to look on the positive side. I have few moments these days when there could even be a positive spin. So Hope knows. She hasn't gone around school screaming my shame at the top of her lungs. She doesn't seem to be relishing it, as I assumed she would.

Brady clenches his jaw. "I didn't mean to. She tricked me. I'm actually pretty mad at her."

"How did she do that?" How can someone trick someone into spilling something?

"She could tell something was bothering me and just, she knows me really well. And I don't know. I felt so stupid."

All I can hear him saying is that what's going on with me is bothering him. How could it not? But I wish he would talk to me about it instead of Hope prying it out of him.

"Honestly," I say, "I'm surprised it's taken this long for her to find out, especially with how much her mother helped us in the beginning."

Hope's mom is one of those people who's always willing to help someone in need. It was Brady's parents who confided in her when things started to fall apart. She came to our aid when we were moving into the trailer and even made us some dinners our first month on our own. Mrs. Kaplan seemed to crave the opportunity to take care of us.

"It's totally okay, really," I assure Brady. "Plus, Hope's your closest friend."

"A friend who tricked me."

"Are you really mad at Hope?" I didn't think Brady had the capability to get mad at anybody, especially Hope. He's usually pretty relaxed about things.

"I'm annoyed. I feel like I betrayed you."

So his sour demeanor was solely because he was looking out for me. I put my hand on top of his. "Don't worry about it. Don't get mad at Hope. She was really cool with me, so I guess some good has come of it."

I've never wanted to come between Brady and Hope. I only wish I had that kind of lifelong bond with someone. I used to have that with Hayley. It seems like decades since we would finish each other's sentences and tell embarrassing stories about each other. When she came home from college, we'd spend her first day home in bed, watching old family sitcoms, eating ice cream from the container, and dissecting our current crushes or boyfriends. Our parents were more than happy to have us both out of their hair for a day.

"So what else is going on?" I ask Brady, grateful that his odd behavior has been solved.

"Not much." He starts up the car. "You working today?"

"No. I get today off since I had to work a double on Monday."

"Okay. I'll take you home then."

Relief flows through me as things are getting back to normal between us. That's all I want: to hold on to the normal parts of my life for as long as I can.

He rests his hand on my knee and I feel everything righting itself, until Brady turns the car away from his home. I assumed when he said *home* he meant his house. I haven't been there in over a week. It's going to be freezing back in the trailer, but I don't want to force myself on him. I'll give Brady the time he needs and try once again to look at the positive side: I could use a couple of hours of peace at home to catch up on homework, since I have to tutor and work tomorrow.

"So what are you going to do with your time now the club's over?" I ask him.

He shrugs. "It's nice not to have that stress anymore. I was getting burned out on it anyway."

I place my hand on top of his. "I can think of someone who wouldn't mind some extra Brady time."

He squeezes back. "I'm not feeling that great, babe. Give me a day or two to rest, but I'll pick you up tomorrow."

"Okay," I reply, my voice tiny.

There's something still wrong with Brady. If it isn't him divulging to Hope, what could it be?

We spend the rest of the short ride not really speaking. When he takes the turn to our trailer, I spot Hayley's car in front.

Brady breaks the silence. "I thought Hayley would be at work."

"Me too." My plans for a quiet afternoon are ruined. Maybe I should call Lila to see if she can pick me up after basketball practice? I can't spend an entire afternoon with Hayley.

Brady finally looks at me, his brows knit in concern. "Are you going to be okay?"

No. I'm not going to be okay. I haven't been okay in a really long time. But there are certain battles I need to face on my own. Brady's had to do enough. I should be able to do something as simple as be in the same trailer as my sister.

"Of course!" I reply as I get out of the car.

I give Brady a big smile as I wave good-bye. I take a deep breath as I open the trailer door, wondering what's waiting for me inside.

The trailer is dark, the curtains drawn. Hayley is lying on the couch/my bed with sunglasses on her face, an empty McDonald's bag in front of her. She's watching some talk show with the volume low.

"I thought you had to work," she says to me without even glancing my way.

"I have the afternoon off." I stand there, not really sure

where to go. There aren't a lot of options and she's currently taking up the only space in the trailer that's mine.

She lights a cigarette.

"Can you please not smoke on my bed?" I ask.

"*Can you please not smoke,*" she mimics me in a high, annoying voice. "You're such a saint." She blows the smoke directly onto my sleeping bag.

"Why aren't you at work?"

"Not feeling well," she replies, although I suspect it's not a cold that has her down, but a hangover. This isn't the first time I've seen her in this condition. "Besides, I've decided my talents are better served elsewhere."

"What does that mean?"

She pushes the sunglasses up to her forehead—her eyes are red and watery. "It means, baby sister, I got sacked. Bunch of thankless ingrates. Like it's such a pleasure to serve and clean up after drunken buffoons."

I lean against the trailer door, taking in the weight of what she's telling me. "You got fired?"

There is no positive side of this scenario. It's a disaster. There's no way I can float us by myself. Hayley needs a job. Not solely to help pay the bills, but because part of the condition of her guardianship is that she must remain employed. The social worker was never thrilled Hayley was working at a bar, but at least she was earning a steady paycheck on top of tips.

Hayley puts her sunglasses back on and turns the volume up on the TV. "I figure I can take some time off since you have a nice cushy tutoring gig. Let's face it, the only reason I'm stuck in this hellhole is because of you."

"*We're* stuck in this situation because of Mom and Dad," I remind her, even though I don't have the fight in me to defend myself. I'm tired of this conversation. I'm tired of arguing with her. I'm tired of it all. "Do you think that I want to live like this? Your attitude is making it worse."

She stabs her cigarette out on my sleeping bag. "Yes, because a sunny disposition will make all this go away. I'm only one smile away from the heat working! And if I think of unicorns and rainbows, the rent will magically be paid!"

"Hayley, please," I beg, desperately wishing my sister would resurface from the pool of negativity sitting in front of me. "We can make this better. We simply have to work a little harder."

"I'm sick of working. I'm sick of having to take care of you." Her voice is emotionless and distant.

"When was the last time you've done anything for me?" I scream. Tears start welling up behind my eyes. "I don't even know who you are anymore. I'm in this by myself."

"Please, poor you," she spits back at me. "You have Lila and Brady. How are those free handouts you get on a daily basis? What about *me*? I have nobody looking out for me. Let's tell it like it is: You have everything, while I have nobody. Period."

"That's not true—you have me." She does. Even though I've tried to be as far away from Hayley as possible the last few months. It breaks my heart she feels that way, but she never spent a lot of time in this town when we still had a normal life. When we moved here, she was already in college and only came to visit during the holidays. She didn't know anybody here except our parents and my friends. She spent summers at school, taking a couple of classes and staying at her sorority house. She never really made a home here before she was forced to move back. "We're in this together."

She laughs coldly. "Spare me. You're planning on ditching this place the second you graduate."

"But you can leave, too! What about college? What about planning for a future?" I press her. It's a conversation I've tried to have with her many times in the past, but she always shuts me down.

"I have no future."

"Hayley—"

She cuts me off. "I'm so tired of you thinking that you're better than me. You're a spoiled little princess who has ruined my life. I hate you."

Tears are starting to fall down my cheeks. "You don't mean that."

She stands up. There is so much anger in her face. For the first time, I'm truly scared. I always knew I'd be able to handle school and work, but I can't lose the only family member I have left. I can't have her also abandon me.

"I do," she says. "I hate you and wish you were never born. GET OUT!" She points to the door. "GET THE HELL OUT OF HERE! I never, and I mean *never*, want to see you again."

I quickly turn around and leave the trailer, slamming the door behind me. I'm fully sobbing now. I look around the trailer park, wondering where I can go, who I can call.

I'm three miles from downtown. I do the only thing I can think of and start walking.

Lila's at practice. Things with Brady are too fragile. My sister hates me.

I really am on my own.

"Want another slice?" Peter offers as I wait in The Pie Shoppe for Lila.

"Thanks," I reply as he places another plain slice in front of me.

"What aren't you telling me?" He tilts his head to the side. Peter knows about my situation. But he, like everybody else in my life, remains clueless about Hayley. "I can tell something's bothering you. Brady?"

"No, my sister and I got into a fight. It's nothing," I lie, because it's everything.

How can I ever go back there after she said all those hateful things to me? How can things ever be the same?

What hurts most is that even though things have been tense with Hayley, she's stayed. She wasn't like Mom and Dad, who bailed. What is it about me that makes people want to leave?

I start to sniff. I grab a napkin from the metal holder on the table and blow my nose. I can't start sobbing in front of Peter. He can't know the truth. The real truth. Nobody can.

"Great," I say with a forced laugh. "And now I think I'm catching her cold."

That's the lie I told Lila: My sister has the flu and I don't want to get sick. It should buy me a few days before her parents start asking questions about why I haven't gone home.

Home. Like I know what that is anymore. Maybe I can convince Lila's parents to let me stay long-term. Maybe I can take the GRE and then leave. But I don't have enough money for college yet.

"You know I'm here for you if you need anything," Peter offers.

"I know, I appreciate it. You don't have to worry about me—just a bad day." I've had plenty of bad days, but this day is more than bad. It's the apocalypse of my world as I know it.

"Order's up," Tiffany, the other waitress, informs Peter as he excuses himself to the kitchen.

I finish up the rest of my homework right as Lila arrives. "Hey!" she greets me. "Sorry to hear about Hayley. You ready to go?"

"Yes." I take my plate and utensils to the back and say good-bye to Peter. When I return to the front, Lila's looking around my booth.

"Where's your bag?" she asks.

"What bag?"

"Um, you're going to be staying with us for a few days— didn't you pack a bag?"

I laugh as I smack my head. "I'm such a ditz sometimes. I totally forgot."

Yet, I never forget things. I can't afford to be careless, but here I am. I planned everything out on my walk into town. But I hadn't thought it totally through. Who would plan a few days away from home without packing a bag?

"No problem. We can drive to your house and pick it up."

Panic flashes through me. "It's okay. I have some clothes at your house. I'll go tomorrow to get the rest of my things." Although I know I can't go back to the trailer. Not tomorrow. Maybe never again.

I didn't think about the bag because it's such an insignificant thing. What's the point of having some personal items if you no longer have a family or a home?

450 DAYS LEFT

There were many times when I had no idea how I was going to get through something. But there was always a part of me that knew everything would eventually be okay.

I don't think that anymore.

While walking the hallway between classes, I try to let the monotony of going to class, opening up my books, and eating lunch steady my nerves. All last night, I had to convince Lila's parents that Hayley didn't need them to bring her anything. That's the last thing I need—for anybody to see the shape she's in.

When Brady texted me this morning to inform me he wasn't feeling well and wouldn't be at school today, I felt relieved. I didn't need his aloofness as another reminder of how much things have turned upside down.

"Hi, Parker!" Hope greets me in the hallway, a big smile on her face.

"Hey," I reply as she falls in step with me.

"Looking forward to our session after school. I think I'm going to ace my next test!"

"That's great." I force myself to return a smile, when it's the last thing I want to do right now. While I appreciate her effort to be civil, I don't want her kindness simply because she feels sorry for me. I want people to like me for me, not my circumstances. Just like I want my sister to love me because we're family, not because she's been ordered by the court to be my guardian.

The static of the speakers crackles in the hallway as the assistant principal requests that I come to the office.

"Is everything okay?" Hope asks with wide eyes.

I shrug. "I'm sure it's nothing." I give her a tiny wave as I turn the corner to the office, but freeze in my tracks when I see Sheriff Moore standing in the office with my social worker.

They've found Dad. Or Mom.

That has to be it.

I've never put much thought into what would happen if they ever found either of them. I never even think much about my parents anymore. At first I'd try to figure out where they were or imagine what they were doing. But then I gave up. It didn't really matter, did it? It's not as if you can force people to be parents. Of course, there's always court-mandated child support, but you can't force someone to love another person.

I walk into the office with my heart in my throat. "Hi, Sheriff Moore, Ms. Bremner."

Sheriff Moore takes his hat off. "Why don't we step into the principal's office so we can have some privacy."

I nod as they guide me inside.

Ms. Bremner sits next to me and places her hand on my shoulder. "It's your sister."

"What's wrong?" I ask even though I already know they know. It's a small town—of course they found out she'd been fired from her job. They would have to give her some time to find another job, not as if that would fix my personal issues with her.

"First, you need to know she's going to be fine," Ms. Bremner says as she exchanges a glance with the sheriff. "She's in the hospital. A friend stopped by late last night and Hayley wasn't answering the door, even though he could see she was in the trailer. She was unresponsive so he called an ambulance. Your sister had alcohol poisoning."

My face remains blank. I don't know how to process this information. At a certain point the human mind has to reach its capacity for horrible news. There's a buzzing in my ears as I feel myself shutting down, emotionally and maybe even physically.

Ms. Bremner continues, "We were informed this morning of her condition. Listen, Parker, we have a lot of questions about your care. But right now, we'll take you to see her. She's awake now, a little worse for wear, but she will be fine."

I look at my hands, clasped tightly in my lap. I know the adults are expecting me to say something. I feel as if I have no other option but to finally admit the truth, as much as it hurts.

"I don't think she wants to see me," I say.

"Parker, when was the last time you were in the trailer?" Sheriff Moore inquires. "When we went to inspect it, the heat wasn't working, it smelled of cigarette smoke, and it appeared as if you haven't been there in a while."

"I spent last night at a friend's, but I spend most nights at the trailer," I reply in a nearly robotic voice. This can't be happening.

"As you know, Hayley's guardianship is contingent on her holding a job and providing suitable living quarters for you. None of those requirements are currently being met. Quite frankly, she's in no condition to be your guardian."

I nod, because there's no getting around it anymore. It was only a matter of time before social services found out about Hayley. I was fooling myself in thinking I could get away with it. That I could hold on for the next 450 days until I could leave town with my diploma and college scholarship in hand.

Ms. Bremner gives the sheriff a warning look. "These are all things we can discuss later. But, Parker, you know we're here for you. You should've said something."

I know I should've, but then what? I'd get pulled out of the trailer and sent with some foster family. I've contemplated filing for emancipation, but that takes a lawyer, which requires money. Even if I were considered a legal adult, I'd still have to find somewhere to stay. That also costs money.

There's a price to everything: freedom, and now, admitting the truth. Although I have yet to fully understand what the cost will be of the revelation about Hayley, I do know one thing: I won't be able to afford it on many levels.

Ms. Bremner puts her arm around me. "Let's go see your sister."

I want to object, but I'm worried about Hayley. She's my family. I didn't inherit the gene from my parents that allowed them to turn off the ability to care. There's also a gnawing idea that's been growing in my head that this is my fault. That our fight prompted her to drink even more than usual.

Sheriff Moore holds open the door for me as I exit the office, grateful everybody is in class so nobody witnesses me being escorted off the premises by the police.

Nobody likes hospitals.

What's to like? The bright fluorescent lights, the cold linoleum floor, the sickness and death wafting through the air?

Ms. Bremner takes me to Hayley's room. There's a privacy curtain between her and an older man sleeping with his mouth open. The only noise in the room comes from his snores and the machine beeping next to him.

Hayley looks so tiny in her bed. She has an IV in her arm, dark circles around her eyes, and her hair appears darker since it's been pulled away from her face. It looks as if she hasn't had a proper shower in days. Probably because she hasn't. I didn't even think about how no heat affected our hot water. I've been showering at Lila's.

"Hayley," I whisper. My chin starts to tremble. This is my fault. I shouldn't have said anything to her yesterday. I should've simply sat on the floor, done my homework, and kept my mouth shut.

Hayley opens her eyes. When she sees me, she turns over on her side with her back to me. I look at Ms. Bremner for a hint about what I'm supposed to do. Not only with my sister, but with my life.

"I'll leave you two to have some privacy," she says as she gives me a pat on my arm.

I cautiously walk over to the other side of the bed so Hayley has no choice but to see me. "Hayley, are you okay?"

She laughs. "Of course not. Do I look okay?"

"Who found you?"

"Evan."

I guess I should be grateful to him for calling an ambulance, but it should've been me. I should've been there for her. I'm all she has.

"Oh, Hayley." My voice rises because I can no longer control my emotions. Tears start flooding down my face. I fall on my knees and wrap my arms around my sister. "I'm sorry! I'm sorry I said those things to you. I'm sorry you're stuck here because of me. I'm sorry I ruined your life."

Hayley starts shaking as she finally lets go of everything pent up inside her. "It's not your fault. I did this to myself. What are we going to do?"

My sister and I hold on to each other tightly, making us one unit. One miserable and crying unit.

What *are* we going to do? I don't know. I have absolutely no idea.

"We'll figure it out," I tell her.

Neither Hayley nor I put ourselves in this situation. Our dear old parents did this to us. We've been left to pick up the pieces. We survived that, and we'll survive this. We have to—there aren't any other options for us.

"I messed everything up, didn't I?" she asks, her voice small.

"No. I'll talk to Ms. Bremner—the most important thing is for you to get better. For you to get help."

"How much is all this going to cost?"

I hadn't even thought about the monetary costs of all this, only the emotional. We have Medicaid, but we'll still have to pay something for her stay in a hospital. I heard Sheriff Moore and Ms. Bremner talking on the ride over. Hayley will need to go into counseling or some kind of rehab. There's no way they'll let me stay with her unless she completes some program.

"I'll take care of it," I promise her as I gently stroke her hair, something I've often seen caring mothers do on TV. Our parents weren't affectionate people, but I want to comfort Hayley, and in a way, comfort myself. "You focus on getting better."

All I can do now is hold on to the hope she'll get help and maybe, hopefully, this will turn her around and she'll reclaim her life.

"I'm sorry," Hayley weeps.

"Me too." I hold my sister tightly. No matter what the future holds, I will be here for her. She gave up her life as she knew it when she came back for me.

Now it's time for me to take care of her.

"Parker." Ms. Bremner knocks on the door to Hayley's room. "You have a visitor."

I look at the clock. I've only been at the hospital for less than an hour, but have spent most of it wrapped around my sister. She needs to know she's not alone. We're going to get through this together.

Together. Like how most families handle hardships.

"I'll be right back." I kiss Hayley on her forehead.

I walk out into the hallway, not sure who would be here to see me except Ms. Bremner or a police officer.

I hardly get a chance to process who it is because she's hugging me so tightly the second I exit the room. "Parker, hon, how are you doing?"

"Mrs. Kaplan?" I'm stunned. My arms are limp around my sides, trying to figure out not only why she's here but how she even found out.

She releases her grip and puts her hands on my shoulder as she examines me. "Are you okay?"

I nod. "I'll be fine."

"Hope called and said you might need me."

Hope called? *Hope?* She must've seen me leave school with the police. But still, she called her mom?

"Sweetie, you don't need to do this on your own." She holds my hands as she turns her attention to Ms. Bremner. "What can I do to help? What does Parker need? What does Hayley need?"

"We'll be fine," I assure her.

"Parker." Mrs. Kaplan places her hands gently on my face. "You do not need to do this alone. Please let me help."

All I can do is nod. In what seems like my current default setting, I begin to cry, tears streaming from my eyes. I find myself sinking down to the floor, the exhaustion getting the best of me. Mrs. Kaplan sits on the floor with me and rocks me back and forth as I let it all go. This has been too much. The last year has been too much. Clearly, Hayley and I need help.

What we really need is a mom.

Ms. Bremner starts explaining the situation to Mrs. Kaplan. "Bottom line: Hayley is going to need to complete an alcohol program and get a job before Parker can live with her again. In addition, the residence must get back to a proper living condition."

"Parker will stay with us for as long as she needs," Mrs. Kaplan says without hesitation. "We have an extra bedroom for her. Hope can take her to school. I can contact our lawyer to make arrangements and whatever requirements we need to do. We'll take care of it."

My first thought: *Thank you, Mrs. Kaplan, for stepping up when we need someone the most.*

My second: *Hope is absolutely going to hate this plan.*

"What about Hayley?" I ask, not wanting to leave her alone, especially in that trailer.

"We're going to hold her for the night and figure out what kind of treatment she'll need," Ms. Bremner says. "There are a few programs we'll look into. When she gets back, we'll assist her in getting a job. When she's proven to be stable, we can discuss incorporating you back in."

"But she's my sister—I can't leave her."

"What's best for both of you right now is for Hayley to get help. You'll be able to visit her."

"How long before I can move in when she gets back? Days? Weeks?" I've spent the last year devising a plan to get out of that trailer, out of this town. Now all I want is to get back there as soon as possible.

Ms. Bremner looks at Mrs. Kaplan. "I'm not going to lie. It may be months."

I turn to Mrs. Kaplan. "I can't stay with you for months. I'll talk to Lila's parents—"

Mrs. Kaplan cuts me off. "Hon, you are welcome to stay as long as you want. It's not a problem. In fact, I insist. I know you're used to being on your own, but I want to help you."

She does. She always has. That's the kind of person Mrs. Kaplan is. But it's not fair to Hayley that she's going to be stuck in some program while I'm being spoiled rotten by Hope's mom.

A mom. I look at Mrs. Kaplan. I've always ached for a mom like her. Someone who's selfless and caring. I get to have it, even for a brief moment of time. Hope's bound to resent me for it, but she's had this life for sixteen years. All I want is a few days of not having to do everything on my own. To have someone who cares.

Maybe being around Mrs. Kaplan will show me how I need to be when Hayley gets back. I can be that person for her, the one who will take care of things.

I can have the life I've always wanted for a fleeting moment. All I have to do is say yes.

"Hayley will be taken care of?" I ask, wanting to ensure I'm not abandoning my sister.

"Of course," Ms. Bremner confirms.

I look at Hope's mom. Her eyes are filled with concern, her generous heart practically bursting out of her chest.

I squeeze her tightly and exhale a breath I feel I've been holding for over a year.

"Yes."

I know this may sound really crazy with everything going on, but I insisted on going to work.

Mrs. Kaplan dropped me off after we went to the trailer so I could pack up everything I'd need for an extended stay. Peter told me I could take the night off, but with such a huge shift in my life, I wanted desperately to hold on to the only two things that haven't changed for me: school and work.

"I've got something for you," Peter tells me two hours into my shift. I go to the kitchen and see a small pizza loaded with veggies. "You're about due for your break. Head to the back room and enjoy."

"Thanks," I reply as I walk to the small room with a fold-out table and two chairs. It's the first time I've sat down in silence since everything happened with Hayley. I'm going to visit her tomorrow and talk with Ms. Bremner about our options. It's nice we'll have choices for once. We're so used to having things forced on us, having a say in a major decision is a welcome change.

I lean back on the chair as I slowly chew my food, enjoying my break.

There's a knock on the door and I'm stunned when I see Brady standing there.

"Hey," he says sheepishly as he comes over to hug me. "Mrs. Kaplan came over and told my family everything. I'm so sorry."

"Thanks." I wrap my arms around him. His embrace always gives me comfort and makes me feel safe. Maybe things won't be so bad after all. Hayley's going to get help. I've got a warm place to sleep. And Brady appears to be back.

"I've been such a jerk the last couple of days. I'm sorry."

"It's okay."

Ever since everything fell apart, I've realized how often people apologize to me. While the sentiment is appreciated, I sometimes wish people would stop feeling sorry and simply say the truth. How refreshing it would be if people stated the truth about my circumstances: *That totally sucks.*

I feel a little bit of the weight off me now that Brady admits to his distance, but everybody's allowed to have a few days off.

"Are you okay staying with Hope? I know how you two are." He grimaces slightly, probably not thrilled his girlfriend and best friend will be living under the same roof.

I shrug. It's not the Hope part I'm focused on—it's being around her mom. "If I'd realized all it would take for Hope to be nice to me was to know my truth, I would've told her right away. And I don't know if you know this, but Hope was the one who called her mom to help me. I never thought I'd ever be so grateful to Hope Kaplan in my life, but if it wasn't for her, well, I don't know what I would've done."

"You could stay with us."

"You've already done too much."

He has. It's really not fair how much of a burden I've had to be on Brady's and Lila's families. They didn't ask to have to take care of another kid. A night here and there is one thing, but an indefinite amount of time?

"But we can do more."

"Brady, I don't want this to come off the wrong way, but you don't have to worry about it. I would like, if only for a few days, maybe a couple weeks, to be a regular girl, a normal friend and girlfriend. Granted, I'm a regular girl mooching off a family I'm not close with, but I want the stability. I want you not to have to stress over where my next meal will come from. Or if I need a ride. You shouldn't feel like you have to be my guardian. It hasn't been fair to you."

It hasn't been fair to anybody. While I appreciate that he's been so sweet and attentive to me, it will be nice to be a normal couple. I know I'm fooling myself because there's nothing normal about my situation, but for the first time in a year, I'm going to be in a stable living situation.

And for the first time in my life, I'm going to be around a real mom. That's what I'm most excited about. Lila's and Brady's moms have been great. They've been sweet and understanding, but Hope's mom is special. She seems to have this desire to nurture people. Hope appears bothered when her mom tries to take care of her. Mrs. Kaplan isn't going to have any fight from me. I *want* to be taken care of.

Brady thinks over what I have to say about not needing him to take care of me. After a few beats, he takes my hand. "I wouldn't do it if I didn't want to."

I lean into him. "I know."

"Plus . . ." he says before taking a deep breath.

I wait for him to finish his thought, but instead he grinds his teeth. "Plus?" I prod.

His face has a blank look. He quickly shakes his head and smiles. "Nothing. Everything's good, right?"

I don't know how things are going to be tomorrow or next week. Don't even bother asking me about next year. Right now, things are okay. With everything I've been through, okay is more than fine with me.

Five minutes to closing, I'm wiping down the tables when the front door dings. I let out a little sigh. It's the worst when someone comes right before we close and orders a pizza.

I put on my best smile as I turn around to greet the customer, hoping they're picking up an order. It's Hope, holding her car keys. "Hey, I told Mom I'd pick you up."

"Oh." I haven't seen her since it was decided I'd be staying there. "That's great. It's still going to be a couple minutes. Is that okay?"

"Of course." She slides into a booth. "Take your time."

"Do you want a Cherry Coke? On the house!" It's nice to finally offer her something, even if it's more of a gesture than anything of real substance.

She shakes her head. "If I have too much sugar before bed, I'll never get to sleep."

I let out a nervous laugh. I'd be fooling myself if I thought this wouldn't be an awkward situation, but Hope comes with Mrs. Kaplan. I'll make the best out of it as I can. That's all I've ever been able to do.

I finish the rest of my closing duties in record time. "Okay to head out, boss?" I ask Peter.

"Since when are you friends with that Kaplan girl?" His memory of that disastrous Valentine's Day is about as fresh as mine.

"Long story," I reply. Then I realize that maybe it's time for him to know the whole truth. "I'll tell you all about it, the next time we're slow."

"You take care," he says with a nod.

"I'm ready," I declare to Hope, who's busy typing into her phone. I wonder what she's told Madelyn. Oh God, I didn't think about the fact I'll have to be around *her* as well. But maybe she'll soften on me since I'll be living with her best friend. Hope has seemed to. Not like she currently has a choice, but still.

We walk out of the store with Peter locking the door

behind us. "So . . ." I let that word hang in the air as I try to decide what exactly to say to Hope. "I can't begin to even tell you how much this means to me. I'm really glad you called your mom and I hope it's not too weird I'm staying with you. I'll try not to get in the way. I appreciate the offer so much. Things have been really crazy. I know Brady told you some stuff and if you have any questions simply let me know. But needless to say, it hasn't been a good year. Probably the understatement of the decade." I'm talking so fast, not realizing how nervous I am until the words begin spewing from my mouth.

Hope pauses in front of her car. I go to the other side, waiting for her to unlock the door, but she's still. She finally looks at me. "I'm really sorry about how I've acted toward you."

There's that *sorry* again. Although in Hope's case, the apology is probably a little overdue.

She goes on. "I had you all wrong. And it's kind of made me look at myself differently and, well, I know I've been an entitled brat. I'll try to be better."

"I really appreciate that. And you've done enough, believe me. Letting me into your house, well, it's the kindest thing anybody's done for me. Thank you."

Hope smiles at me, an actual genuine smile. I've seen her smile countless times, but never at me. She's so pretty when she does. Her entire face lights up.

"Okay, Parker." She unlocks the car. "Let's go home."

Home. It's not my home. It never will be my home, but for the next little while I get to have a place to call home. A place where the door is open for me. Where I'm wanted.

It's such a simple thing to take for granted, until you've had it taken away from you.

446 DAYS LEFT

I've gone from living a nightmare to living in a dream.

It's been four nights since I started living with the Kaplans. Every morning when I wake up under a warm duvet in my own king-size bed, I think, *This can't be real life*. I pad my feet over the plush carpeting in my bedroom to heated tile in my own bathroom, and come downstairs to find breakfast and, more important, a family waiting for me.

I can't believe people actually live like this.

"Good morning, Parker!" Mrs. Kaplan greets me on Monday morning. "It's breakfast burrito day. Do you want sausage or bacon in your burrito? Orange juice or cranberry juice?"

"I can help myself," I tell her, although it's a losing battle. Mrs. Kaplan loves waiting on her family. It got to a point with Lila's family where they would let me clear the dinner table and do the dishes. I wanted to somehow earn my keep, even though I can never repay the kindness that has been given to me.

"Nonsense! You sit down. Did you get a good night's sleep?"

"Yes, a wonderful night's sleep." I've slept so much since I've been here. I'm making up for months of lost sleep. "Thanks again."

"Of course, hon." Mrs. Kaplan puts a steaming burrito in front of me.

"Good morning! How are my girls this morning?" Mr. Kaplan walks into the kitchen with a smile on his face as he kisses his wife on the cheek. I think it's sweet how affectionate the Kaplans are toward each other. My parents never showed any affection—it was more like a business relationship than a loving marriage. I'd always assumed married couples that kiss and still love each other after all these years was fiction created to sell anniversary cards and romantic movies.

Mr. Kaplan pours himself a big cup of coffee. It's funny, now that I have unlimited access to caffeine, I don't need it as much anymore. It's amazing how much a good night's sleep changes you.

"Did you sleep well, Parker?" Mr. Kaplan asks.

"Yes, thanks." It's so foreign to have people actually want to know about me. Of course, inquiring about my sleep is a pretty simple question, probably more of politeness than anything. However, it's refreshing to be with people who do care. Who don't ignore me.

"Hope!" Mrs. Kaplan yells up the stairs. "Your breakfast is getting cold. Hurry up!"

I'll never understand why Hope basically has to be dragged down the stairs every morning. If this were my reality, I'd be on time for breakfast with my parents every day. Although, she doesn't know any different. This attention is most likely seen as an inconvenience to her.

If she only knew. But I think she does now. She hasn't snapped at her mom since I've been here. She's more thoughtful around me before she speaks. And she's been really cool about me staying. It's not as if we've become best friends, far from it, but she's being civilized and that's all I can ask for.

"Morning," Hope says as she rubs her eyes.

I try not to laugh that she's tired. She has no idea what tired is.

"Morning!" I give her a smile. I'm not so embarrassed about my teeth anymore. At least I don't feel like I have to hide myself, my real self, from Hope.

"Sweetie, do you want a burrito, or only the insides? I can't remember if you're eating carbs this week."

Hope grimaces at her mom. "I'll have the burrito."

"Fabulous!" She starts dishing out the eggs, cheese, bacon, salsa, and guacamole into a flour tortilla.

This is what she does for a Monday morning. On Friday, my first morning, she made Belgian waffles with different toppings. This weekend, Mrs. Kaplan wanted to introduce me to the cuisine she grew up on and made a huge Mexican breakfast on Sunday with chilaquiles, huevos rancheros with spicy salsa, and pan dulce. I ate it all.

It should come as no surprise that Mrs. Kaplan also makes delicious lunches for Hope and me to take to school. At first I declined, worried if I didn't use my lunch subsidy it would be taken away from me. As much as I'm enjoying this time at the Kaplans', it's not forever. I'll eventually move back with Hayley and need my security blankets.

Fortunately, I'll be able to go back on the program once I'm home. So for now, I get to take these wonderful lunches with me every day. I can't even begin to say how much of a relief it is to know where my next meal is coming from. I haven't had that in a year. It's something so many of my friends don't even think about—they have a family; they'll get a meal.

As much as I enjoy eating well and sleeping in a warm bed, I miss my real family, Hayley. I realize it's fairly ironic that now, when she's not here, is when I really appreciate her.

She's only an hour away at a rehab facility. I can visit her next weekend. She'll be out in a month. Upon her release, she has to get a stable job, fix up the trailer, and then the state will decide whether or not I'll be able to return.

I want to return. The trailer isn't great, but it's our home, for better or for worse. Hayley and I are still in this together. We can't let Mom and Dad win.

"Ready for your exam?" I ask Hope.

She nods. "Yes, thanks for grilling me last night."

"Thank *you*," I reply.

I'd take saying *thanks* a million times over having to say or hear another *sorry*.

Hope glances at the clock. "We should leave in five." She takes another bite of her burrito before she heads back upstairs.

I have everything ready. My school bag was packed before I went to bed last night. I'd gotten used to making quick exits in the morning.

"Here's your lunch, Parker." Mrs. Kaplan hands me a bright, polka-dotted, insulated lunch bag. "On today's menu: rotisserie-chicken-salad sandwich on focaccia, carrots and hummus, and a homemade brownie I whipped up last night."

"Sounds amazing." I'm starting to look forward to lunch now. "Thanks again."

I have a huge grin on my face, probably the biggest I've had in a year. I'm so incredibly grateful. I've been dealt a crappy deck of cards, but I'm starting to think I'll at least break even. For the first time since things with Hayley started to fall apart, there's a chance I might get out of this mess.

"Brady's here!" Hope calls from the stairs.

I put my jacket on, grab my school bag and lunch. Mr. and Mrs. Kaplan kiss Hope good-bye and Mrs. Kaplan gives me a hug. "Have a great day at school," Mr. Kaplan says to us as we walk outside and get into Brady's car.

"Good morning," Brady greets us as I get in the front seat, while Hope gets in the back.

We did this Friday morning and again today. I don't know why we never carpooled before, since Hope and Brady live so close together.

Actually, I think I know why.

"How was your morning?" Brady asks.

"Great."

It really was. I haven't had to tell a lie since I moved in with the Kaplans. The last couple of days have been amazing. I still have my routine of work and school, but now I get a new routine of a stable home and regular meals.

Bit by bit, I feel my guard coming down.

One benefit of having a real home and getting a good night's sleep: more time for my friends.

"I missed you this weekend," Lila says to me Thursday after school as we grab a quick bite before she has practice and I have to work.

"But now we can make actual weekend plans that don't involve me mooching off your family," I argue.

"You were never a mooch," Lila replies with a shake of her head. "I still can't believe you're living with Hope Kaplan."

"I know, but it's been nice. *She's* been nice. I think I was wrong about Hope." I never disliked Hope, but I always knew she didn't like me because of Brady. Therefore, I tried to stay away from her as much as possible. She never bothered to get to know the real me, same way I never tried to truly know her. She's been mature enough to admit she was wrong about me and I'll return that gesture by being understanding about where she was coming from. Besides, she's more than made up for it now.

"Has Madelyn been by yet?" Lila asks with a terrified look on her face.

"No, Hope goes to her. I don't know if Hope's embarrassed by me or doesn't want Madelyn near me, but all I know is I'm grateful I don't have to have her glare at me in that house. I get it enough at school. The Kaplans' house is my safe space."

"So," Lila says as she sits up taller in her chair at the coffee shop. "Since you're totally a regular teenager now."

"Yes, completely boring and drama free—it's wonderful!"

"We need to discuss another double date with Conor and Brady. This weekend? When are you working?"

"I'm free Saturday night. I'll check with Brady later."

"Things good with you guys?"

"I think so. He was weird for a bit, but ever since I've been at the Kaplans' things have returned to normal."

"You're so, so normal now," Lila teases. She finishes her latte, while I take a sip of my green tea, one of the cheapest things on the menu. Even though I don't have to spend money on food now, I'm not going to waste it. I still have a long way to go to afford college, and the deductible for Hayley's hospital and rehab stints has set me back a bit, but you can't put a price on sisters. "Do you want me to drop you off at The Pie Shoppe?"

"No, I don't have to be there until five. Do you mind taking me to Hope's? I need to get some homework done before work."

"Of course. Homework and work. How predictable your life has become."

It's true and I absolutely love it.

You get used to the circumstances you've been given. I never realized how much where I lived affected me. But it only takes me a fraction of the time to get my homework done when I'm in a quiet house.

The only noise I hear when I'm working on calculus is a car pulling into the driveway and the front door opening. I figure it's either Hope or her mom. I wait to finish the last couple of equations before I head downstairs to let whoever know I'm home.

I lie down on the bed after I'm done to simply enjoy this moment. Homework is done. I'm going to work tonight. Things will be okay.

After eating the rest of the apple I brought up, I take the plate with me as I start to walk downstairs. I pause every couple of seconds to dig my toes into the carpeting. I always wore shoes in the trailer. The floors were dirty and often sticky, no matter how many times I scrubbed the floor. Now I relish the feeling of the soles of my feet on such luxurious ground.

Hope's voice drifts up as I walk down the stairs. Then it gets quiet. Eerily quiet. I turn on the landing to see Hope on the couch with her arms around Brady.

It takes a few moments to process what I'm seeing. But there they are. These best friends for years, in each other's embrace.

"I love you, you know that, right?" Brady says to Hope as I feel the wind get knocked out of me.

"I love you, too."

A sob escapes my throat and they quickly let go of each other. Both looking shocked and incredibly guilty.

"I didn't know you were home," Hope starts to explain right as Brady tells me, "This isn't what it looks like."

Then what is it?

I'm in a haze as I run back upstairs, shove my feet into shoes, and grab my things. Being prepared for a quick escape has come in handy once again.

"Parker," Hope says as she starts climbing the stairs while I zip past her. "You've got this all wrong."

"Do I?" I don't realize how on edge I am until I hear my completely unhinged voice. "All I know is you've wanted Brady for years, and now you have him. So congratulations, Hope, you have everything. And don't you love rubbing it in my face? That's why you wanted me here. To remind me of everything I don't have."

"Babe." Brady grabs my arm, but I pull it away. "Listen to me."

"No!" I yell. I've never yelled at him before, but I can't do this anymore. "I don't want to hear it, Brady. I don't need to have explained to me what my eyes have seen."

I race out of the house and start running. I hear my name being called out by both Brady and Hope, but I don't want to listen to what they have to say. After a few blocks, I take a side street, hoping they won't try to come find me. I need to be left alone. I need to think this through.

This is what I get for letting my guard down: a giant knife in my back. This was Hope's plan all along.

I finally calm down long enough to leave Lila a message on her phone. She's all I have left or it's foster care. I can't go back to the Kaplans' or to Brady's. Hayley's in rehab.

I knew Hope's place was a temporary fix, but I had duped myself into thinking everything was going to work out.

It's time I finally accept the truth:

No matter how much I work, no matter what I do, nothing will ever be okay.

Brady

It's hard to keep a secret in a small town.

I should know. I've been keeping plenty of secrets, which totally sucks. Yeah, there's Parker's big secret, but I've got my own.

Here's one: I'm a horrible person. I know on the outside it looks like I'm this doting, caring boyfriend. At least that's how I try to be. I have to remind myself all the time to do what should come natural when you're The Good Boyfriend: hold hands, touch, kiss, spoil her on holidays. I even call Parker *babe* to remind me of what we're supposed to be.

But what we're supposed to be . . . it's not what we really are. And it feels like my job is to make sure Parker doesn't realize that. She's had to deal with so much crap already—the last thing she needs is to deal with mine.

It just sucks. All of it. I try to not get annoyed at Parker about how I can't have a normal senior year. It's not her fault—of course it isn't. But I busted my butt all through high school to get good grades. I finally got accepted to Purdue, so I should be able to take it relatively easy, but I can't. I'm worrying all the time. I need to be there for her if anything goes wrong, and stuff always goes wrong.

I was completely clueless about how bad things got with Hayley. And here I didn't think I could feel any worse about everything she's going through. When all I want is . . . well, it doesn't matter what I want.

Every time I hear someone in my class talk about senior parties or skipping class, I become jealous. I have to worry about whether or not my girlfriend has enough to eat or if she needs to stay over. I know most guys think I'm this huge stud for having her spend the night, but it's not like that. Nothing is like it seems.

Then there's Hope.

I was so upset that she tricked me into spilling Parker's secret. And that's exactly what she did: She duped me. As mad as I was, I hated being mad at Hope. I'd never had a reason to before Cleveland. But I felt like I let Parker down. I'm always letting someone down, and when I yelled at Hope and saw the look on her face, I knew I'd also let her down. I wasn't the person she thought I was.

Who knew being a clueless idiot and spilling Parker's secret would end up being a good thing? Hope saved Parker. I never thought that would happen. But it gave me a reason to forgive Hope and hang out with her again. I need Hope. When I went to tell her that I forgave her, things were tense for a few minutes, mostly with Hope falling over herself apologizing. Then things just went back to normal with us, because that's how things have always been with Hope. No matter how much time goes by without us talking—because I was in a different school or for nearly an entire month when everything happened with Parker—as soon as we're occupying the same space, it's like no time has passed.

You see, things with Hope are completely the opposite of stuff with Parker. Hope's always been easy to hang with. That kind of happens when you spend your entire life with someone. Yeah, I know she likes me. I have to admit it's flattering and all, but I don't see Hope that way. She's like my little sister.

"Looks like you're stuck with me," Hope says after school on Thursday as we walk to the parking lot. It's weird not to have Parker with us, but she's off somewhere with Lila. Since she moved in with the Kaplans, I don't have to worry about her. The pressure simply went away. I should enjoy just being boyfriend and girlfriend, but that's the problem. Now there isn't a reason for us to be together.

"Brady?" Hope's voice brings me back to the present. "Geez, don't be too thrilled that it's just you and me." She grimaces. Two weeks ago, she would've been legitimately annoyed that my thoughts were with Parker. Now she's simply teasing about my inability to juggle more than one thought.

"Yeah, it's torture," I reply as I nudge her playfully. I know I probably shouldn't touch Hope as much as I do, but it's natural. Everything with Hope is natural. That's how it should be between best friends. Yeah, it should also be the same with my girl, but it isn't.

Here's another truth I'm willing to share: I miss the club. I'm still bummed that after all the work we did and the hours we put in, we only got fourth place. It wasn't even close. These other people used all these mechanics we didn't even think of. One used a lever to strike a match to heat something in a beaker that filled the balloon with steam. Another used a helium pump. We were way out of our league. I keep thinking that if I could've just spent more time on the machine and didn't have . . . other things to worry about, we could've done better.

Hope blushes at my nudging. I feel a bit guilty she's probably getting her hopes up, but she will always mean more to me than some girl I dated. I think about all the times she's helped me. I hardly even talk to any of my old girlfriends or crushes anymore. Hope will be in my life for a really long time.

"Hey." I fling my arm over Hope's shoulder (yeah, I know I should stop, but it's Hope and I never learn). "I can't even begin to tell you how much I appreciate your family helping out Parker. It's been a huge relief knowing she's taken care of."

Hope laughs. "I know, but it's not a big deal. You know that my mom loves fussing over people. She's in heaven. She's been cooking so much, Parker's going to get fat."

I doubt that. As much as I love Hope, it annoys me when she talks like she's fat. She's so obsessed with that stuff. She isn't fat. Although I can't tell her she's got a pretty hot bod. I mean, I guess I could, but it would give her such the wrong idea. I've got enough girl drama already.

"Hey, Hope, this is going to sound really cheesy," I say as I think about everything that's going to happen in the next six months. I don't know why, but I always seem to think about leaving whenever I'm around her. Maybe it's because when I go to Purdue I'm leaving behind my entire life here. I have seventeen years of memories with Hope. A future that she won't be part of seems weird.

She stops walking and cocks her head to the side. "Oh, I can't wait. You think you're some tough guy, but I know what's up."

"Okay, first, when have I ever pretended to be some muscle dude?"

"Point taken." Hope gives me this smile she's perfected over the years, part come-hither, part teasing. "Do go on."

"Promise me you'll take care of Parker next year. Or your mom."

Hope's grin falls. She looks at me with a serious face. "Of course."

"Yo, Team Knights in Shining Armor!" Conor's voice rings across the parking lot. "What are you guys doing right now?"

"Nothing," I reply. "Why?"

Conor catches up to us and pulls out his phone. "We never celebrated Cleveland. And don't go grumbling about fourth place. It's better than fifth or sixth. As Tolkien once wrote, 'I will not walk backward in life.' I'm texting Dan right now. Let's grab a bite to eat."

"Sounds great, and long overdue," Hope replies.

"Yeah, man, that'd be great."

These days I take anything that will get my mind off the mess I created and how I'm going to get out of it.

"To finishing the damn thing!" I hold my glass out to the group as we cheers the fact we did, despite everything, get the machine to work.

"Hear, hear!" Hope replies before she sets her glass down and digs into a piece of pizza.

We went to The Pie Shoppe because there aren't a lot of options in town. It was either this or McDonald's. Parker's boss gave me a dirty look when I walked in. He's been giving me that look ever since Valentine's Day. I know I screwed up. That's always my problem—not thinking things all the way through. I felt bad for Hope and didn't think it was a big deal. But it was.

Sometimes I wonder why Parker would even still want to be with me.

Oh yeah, the whole security-blanket thing. At this point, it has to be the only reason. It's not love, it's comfort.

"Honestly, Hope, I'm a little disappointed in you," Dan says. "One would say that my expectations of you have been let down."

"What are you even talking about?" Hope wads up her napkin and throws it in Dan's face. It bounces off his glasses and lands on his slice.

"Hope has dashed my hope!" Dan continues as he uses the napkin to blot some grease off his slice.

"Ugh," Hope groans. "I'll tell you what—I'm going to miss your scientific and mathematic brain next year, but not your truly awful attempts at puns."

Dan pretends to look scandalized while Hope laughs him off.

"Okay, fair enough." Dan holds his hands out in surrender. "But I had figured your mom would've thrown us some big fete."

"She's been a little preoccupied, but I'll put in a request."

"Yeah, what's going on anyways?" Conor leans back in the booth. "Is Parker staying with you guys or something? She's been spending a lot of time at your house."

My mouth is full of pizza and I try not to react, but we should've had a story ready. People are used to seeing Parker with me so I figured Hope being with us wouldn't raise any red flags.

Hope shrugs. "She's been tutoring me in advanced algebra and staying with us while her family's been away."

"Oh, that's cool." Conor tucks his hair behind his ears. "I didn't really think you guys were friends."

"You'd be surprised by the people I'll slum with. Exhibit A, my present company," Hope fires back. "Dan, have you decided which school you're going with?"

And like that, it's over. I'm always amazed how little it takes to convince people everything's okay with Parker. When was the last time anybody's seen her parents? I think people are desperate to accept partial lies instead of trying to comprehend the whole ugly truth.

Plus, who would believe me? Parker's circumstance is

sort of the kind you have to see in order to believe. How someone could be struggling so much under everybody's noses. Although I shouldn't be surprised people don't know the entire story, because even Parker doesn't know that.

"Should I have my mom throw us a party?" Hope asks as I drive home. "I can't believe I hadn't thought of it. Actually, I'm more in shock she hasn't insisted."

"Like I'd ever turn down a party at your house." I don't know anybody who's ever said no to an invitation from Gabriela. A party at the Kaplans' always means amazing food and an insanely fun time. "But I don't want to put more pressure on your mom."

"Believe me when I say she'd love to."

"Thanks," I reply quietly. I feel like I'm betraying Parker by having these normal moments when everything in her life has been tossed on its side. I will never escape the guilt.

I see Hope studying me out of the corner of my eye. I pull into her driveway, but she doesn't get out of the car.

"Can I ask you a question?"

"Of course." Hope's my best friend. She's never had to ask me for permission to ask a question before. Which automatically makes me stressed.

I shut the car off and turn to Hope.

She studies me for a few seconds. "I'm not sure how to say this, but Parker told me I could ask her any questions about what happened."

"Go ahead," I reply.

"But I only have one question. Something that doesn't make sense, and it's something you said that night in the hotel."

I can feel the lump rising in my throat. Hope has always seen things in me that others can't, but how could she possibly know?

"You said that you've been making things worse. You were so mad at yourself. Why would you even think that? You've been so amazing and supportive of Parker. She wouldn't have survived everything without you."

I feel like I'm going to barf. I can't believe I said that. I was just unloading to Hope, but didn't mean to . . .

Maybe I should just get it off my chest. Maybe things will be better if I admit the truth to somebody. But will Hope ever be able to look at me the same? Will she think it means something it doesn't?

"Brady?" she says as she places her hand on my arm. "You know you can tell me anything. I haven't said a word to anybody about Parker. Not even Madelyn. I don't know how long I can keep Parker staying with us a secret if she's with us more than a few weeks, but I've got Parker's back and you know I've always had yours. No matter what."

I start nodding. It's time to come clean. I shouldn't have this burden on me. It's driving me crazy.

Hope opens the passenger door. "Come inside. My mom's car isn't in the garage. Parker's with Lila. We have the house to ourselves."

"Okay," I say as I get out.

It's time to tell the truth about Parker and me. For once.

. . . .

We enter Hope's house and it's eerily silent. I'm used to the house being alive with people.

I plunk down on the couch. My heart's practically thumping out of my chest.

"What's going on?" Hope asks as she sits right next to me. "I hate seeing you beat yourself up. You haven't done anything wrong."

Isn't living a lie wrong? Isn't doing something entirely out of obligation wrong? Are you really a good guy if you feel like you're only pretending to be a good guy?

I look down at the floor. I know if I don't get this out, the headaches will get worse. That gnawing sensation in the pit of my stomach will get worse.

Just rip the bandage.

"I wanted to break up with Parker."

As soon as I finally admit it, I feel both relieved and awful.

"When?" Hope asks.

And that right there is the problem. The when. The when is why we're still together. Because I have the absolute worst timing in the world.

"Before everything happened, I set up a date with Parker to do it. It was going to be on a Friday. I thought I was being smart by waiting until the weekend. But we never had that date because her dad disappeared."

I went over to her house that Friday, but it wasn't to pick her up for our date. It was to help her pack her bag for

Lila's. She was in a daze. She'd just had her life turned upside down. As much as I wanted to end it, I wasn't going to disappear on her, too. At least not right away.

But things kept going wrong, and that meant there was never a right time. More than anyone else, I could see how hard Parker was working to keep her life in balance. I couldn't be the thing that made it topple.

So I stayed.

And here we are, over a year later.

A year of playing the role of The Good Boyfriend. Of putting everything second to Parker, even after realizing that in another circumstance, we probably wouldn't still be together.

How can I possibly break up with Parker now?

But also . . . how I can keep this up? It's starting to take its toll. But every time I get exhausted from living this lie, I think about everything Parker goes through. And then I just shut up and play the part.

"Oh my God." Hope's voice has a quiver in it. "Why did you want to break up?"

That is a pretty simple answer. "Because even before everything happened, it felt like we weren't on the same wavelength. Because we're both different, but not in compatible ways. I'm a goofball and a nerd, she's super smart and serious. I mean, there are a bunch of reasons. But at the end of the day it came down to the fact that I didn't want to be with her anymore."

"Who did you want to be with?"

And there it is. Why I shouldn't be having this conversation with Hope.

"Nobody," I tell her. "I wanted to be by myself."

Yep. Breaking up with Parker had nothing to do with another girl. It had to do with me. *I* wanted to be single. *I* was happy to spend the rest of my time in high school hanging with my friends. *I* didn't want to be tied down. *I* wanted to have fun.

I feel like a selfish jerk.

"Oh," Hope replies.

I haven't been able to look at her yet. To see how upset she is that I never wanted her to be my girlfriend. To know that I've let her down.

This is my problem: I never want to do anything wrong. I never want to disappoint people. So what do I do? I've stayed with Parker out of pity. And that's not what she wants from me—or from anyone.

We fell into probably the most codependent relationship possible. Parker needs me to feel normal, while I need her to ease my guilt of wanting to break up and live my own life again. I don't even know if Parker would still be with me if her parents hadn't left. So here we are, both trapped with each other, like we've been given the sentence her father had dodged.

I finally look up at Hope. The color has drained from her face. "Brady . . ." she begins, but her voice gives out.

I wait for it. For her to yell at me. For her to tell me that I've led her on. For her to confirm my worst suspicions about myself.

She shakes her head from side to side in a slow, methodical way.

"You can't break up with Parker," she says, then puts her hand over her mouth.

I think we're both shocked by this.

I give up. "I know," I say. "You're right. I'm not going to abandon her, too."

I'm trapped.

But Hope's not done. "You can't lie to her, either," she tells me, her eyes beginning to well up. "She's had enough people in her life lie to her. Oh, Brady, what are we going to do?"

I didn't think it would be possible for me to feel better about what I'm going through. But hearing Hope say *we* makes me feel less alone in this. I need her help. I want to do the right thing. I have been trying to do that for over a year and it keeps burying me deeper and deeper.

"It's going to be okay." Hope wraps her arms around me. "We'll figure something out. You're one of my closest friends."

"Yeah, I'm also the worst."

"No, you're not. Any other guy would've just dumped her and not cared about her feelings. You stayed with her. You gave up a lot of things for Parker. You're one of the good guys, Brady."

I want to believe what Hope's saying. I want to be that person Hope thinks I am.

I wrap my arms around her. "I love you. You know that, right?"

"I love you, too." She hugs me tighter.

I hear a cry that's not from Hope. I look up and see Parker, staring at us with her mouth open. For the second time this afternoon, I feel like I'm going to be sick. What did she hear? How much does she know?

That's when I realize it's what she's seeing that has her so upset: Hope and me with our arms around each other. She thinks we were hooking up.

"This isn't what it looks like," I try to explain while Hope tells her we didn't realize she was here.

Parker dashes up the stairs. We both chase after her, trying to explain we were two friends having a moment. I know what it looked like, but Parker needs to know the truth. And not only what Hope and I were doing, but maybe she really should know everything.

As much as I thought it would help me to tell someone, in the end, the person who really needs to know the truth is Parker.

"Parker." Hope reaches out to her. "You've got this all wrong."

"Do I?" Parker yells. Her face is flush. I've never seen her this angry. Even when her family left her, she stayed relatively quiet, probably out of shock. "All I know is you've wanted Brady for years, and now you have him. So congratulations, Hope, you have everything. And don't you love rubbing it in my face? That's why you wanted me here. To remind me of everything I don't have."

"Babe," I say, the lie slipping so easily off my tongue. I take her by the arm, but she yanks it away from me. "Listen to me."

"No!" Parker says with so much hatred in her voice. "I

don't want to hear it, Brady. I don't need to have explained to me what my eyes have seen."

She runs out of the house and I start to follow her, but Hope grabs my arm. "She needs to calm down. I can explain to her I was having a bad day or something. She'll understand."

"No. I need to talk to her. I don't want to lie to her anymore."

I grab my car keys and head outside to find Parker.

I know there's only one place Parker will go, since Lila is at practice.

Once I turn the corner in the direction of The Pie Shoppe, I see Parker walking quickly, her arms pumping, her hair swinging with every step. I don't have to see her face to know she's angry. She has every right to be, but not for the reason she thinks.

I park a block away, so she doesn't see me coming. I start jogging toward her, not saying anything until I can reach out and gently grab her by the arm.

"Parker," I say softly as she jumps at my touch.

"Leave me alone!" She picks up her pace so she's practically running.

I jog in front of her and place both my hands on her forearms. "Please listen to me. Listen to what I have to say and then you can ignore me forever. Please."

She reluctantly stops. "You know, this serves me right. Here I was stupidly thinking everything was going to be okay. That I was going to get through this. I have no one."

Her chin trembles and all I want to do is reach out and comfort her, even though that's the last thing she needs from me.

"That's not true."

"Please," she snorts. "I wonder how long until Lila gets sick of me? Or Mrs. Kaplan? What is it about me that makes people want to run away? What is it?" The tears welling in her eyes have started to travel down her cheeks.

I can't be another person abandoning her. But I also can't be another person lying to her.

Even though I don't want to be in a romantic relationship with her anymore, it doesn't mean I don't want to be a part of her life.

"That's not what's going on here, believe me. I'm here for you, Hope's here for you, her family, my family—we're all here for you. That wasn't what it looked like with Hope. Please come to my car and let me take you to my house or Hope's house so we can talk."

She folds her arms defiantly. "I'm not going anywhere with you. Say what you have to say or leave."

"Okay." I take a deep breath, but freeze. How can I look her in the face and tell her I don't want to be with her anymore?

"Just tell me what's going on. If you want to be with Hope, fine. Be with Hope. I have a lot bigger problems than my boyfriend cheating on me."

"No, that's not it." I reach out to her, but she pulls away. "Hope's my best friend, period. I'd never cheat on you. You mean a lot to me, Parker. You really do."

"I'm so tired of this, Brady." Parker leans against the brick of the hardware store and slides down to the concrete.

"Aren't things better at the Kaplans'?" I ask, because things had been going better for her the last couple of days. Until I messed everything up.

"Not that. This," Parker says as she gestures between us. "I'm tired of people being with me for the wrong reasons. First, my parents only tolerated me because they had to legally. Then, for a while, Hayley only dealt with me because the court told her she had to. At least things with me and her are getting better. But maybe there are some things that can't be fixed, or at least shouldn't be. I know I relied on you more than I should have. I appreciate everything you've done, but I don't want to be a burden to you, or anyone else, anymore."

I drop down to my knees so I can look her in the eyes. "Parker, you mean the world to me. All I want is to make things better for you. Tell me what I can do. Please tell me what you want."

"What I want?" Parker laughs bitterly. "You can't give me what I want. I want a family. I want a place to call home. I want not to feel as if the rug is always going to be pulled from under me. It doesn't really matter what I want, because I'm never going to get it."

I don't know what to say or do. I can't magically make her family reappear. Plus, her parents weren't great to begin with. I can't give her the kind of home she wants.

"You know what I'd also like?" she asks me. "To not have anybody in my life out of obligation or pity, including you."

"Parker, that's not—" I start to argue.

She cuts me off. "Please don't. Just don't. It's okay. Really."

"What's okay?"

She lets out a little sigh. "I think we're both to blame for staying together as long as we did. As much as I want to put the past behind me, I kept trying to hold on to things. It's like I thought if I appeared normal on the surface, everything that happened in the past wouldn't matter. But it *does* matter. I can't change the past. Nobody can. But I can do something about the future. And what I want for my future is to be truthful. I especially don't want to stay in a relationship that's run its course."

She's giving me an out. She's making this easy on me. But now that it's here, I don't know if I want it.

"But it's not—"

"Brady, stop." She shakes her head. "Let's not lie to each other anymore."

"I want you in my life," I argue. "That's not a lie."

"We can still be friends. I *want* us to be friends." Parker gives me a small smile.

"You do?"

"Of course. You've been so wonderful to me, even if it was out of guilt. But I'm going to be okay."

"I thought you'd hate me if I said I wanted us to stop."

"I don't hate you. I hate my mom and dad."

I've never heard her say that about her parents. I don't blame her.

"You really mean a lot to me, Brady. I know I've come to rely on you and have been a burden. I don't really know what's going to happen. I have no idea what the next hour will bring let alone the next week. I need to take it moment by moment and I think it's time that I do it on my own."

"You don't have to do that." I reach out to touch her knee, but she pulls it away.

"I know I don't have to, but I need to do this. On my own. At least until Hayley gets back."

"Hope's mom really likes having you there. Hope does, too." Things were going great with her and Hope, and then one moment of weakness from me ruins everything.

Huh. I never realized that's basically what Parker's been going through. She hasn't been allowed to have any moments of weakness. Sure, I've seen her get frustrated, but she's sort of just grinned and taken it.

"I know Mrs. Kaplan likes having me there. I don't even doubt Hope's not completely annoyed." She shrugs. "I don't really have a choice in that matter, because the state says I have to remain with them until Hayley is fit to have me move back."

"It's okay to ask for help."

"But that's all I do," she counters. "It's embarrassing. And tiring."

"I know." Although I really have no clue at all what she goes through. I only think I understand what it's like to try to hold things together. I have a family, a home, and a future that's a given.

She gives me a small smile as she stands up. "I need some time to myself."

I don't want to let her go. As much as it's been a burden to be with Parker, there's also a selfish part of me that likes to be needed. "Are you sure you don't want to try again?"

She actually laughs. "No offense, Brady, but my love life is the least of my concerns right now. I've got bigger things to worry about."

How could I have ever thought that us being only friends would break her?

"So you're okay?" I ask, even though I know the answer. If I've learned anything from Parker Jackson, it's that try as her parents, and even Hayley, might, they can't bring her down.

Her gaze is on the road out of town, her eyes not really focusing on anything. Her voice is small, yet assured. "I don't know. I guess . . . it's going to take some time, but eventually, I'll be okay. I have to be. If not for me, for Hayley." She turns away, pauses, and then looks back at me. "I have to believe that things can only get better for me. I deserve that."

She deserves more happiness than anybody I know.

I watch her walk away, even though I want to chase her down and do whatever I can to make things better. But there's nothing I can do.

Parker's right. She's going to be okay. It might be super immature for me to think that, but what other option does she have? To give up? She'd never do that. She has too much fight in her. Look how much she's done to survive so far.

I walk back to my car. I have no idea what the future holds for me. Even though I'd spent the last year wondering how my life would be different without Parker in it, now, as we're walking away from each other, I realize I already miss her. She's been a comfort to me, in her own way. As scary as the thought of going to college in a few months is, the realization that I now have to face the rest of high school without her is unsettling. Any time I'd get overwhelmed about a project or exam, I'd always be reminded, with Parker in the seat next to me, how much she has to deal with. How could I ever really complain when my life is so simple and cushy in comparison?

A smile actually appears on my face. A realization hits me—it's something I don't think Parker even realizes. She saw me as her security blanket, but she didn't need me. She never did, because she always had herself.

Hope

12 DAYS AFTER

This is a disaster of epic proportions.

It makes the *Titanic* look like a relaxing day at the beach.

"Are you okay?" Madelyn asks me as we sit down at the kitchen table.

Parker ran out of here with Brady on her heels, leaving me alone, confused, and hurt. I called Madelyn for an emergency best friend meeting.

Now that she's here, I'm not sure how to answer the simplest question: *Am* I okay?

I don't know. Once I think I know everything, something happens and it gets turned on its side.

"I guess," I reply. I'm not the one who ran out of here because she thinks her boyfriend was cheating. I'm not the one who has nowhere else to go. I'm not the one whose relationship is a lie.

Although I don't know if I can really say that. I've been living a lie when it came to Brady. I had always thought if he wasn't with Parker, he'd be with me. But that's not the truth.

It was never going to be me.

"But all this time . . ." Madelyn presses.

Yes, I've spent years putting off potential relationships because of Brady. Or maybe I've been using that as an excuse to protect myself. It's easier to say I'm not interested than putting myself out there and being rejected.

Although haven't I been rejected by Brady in a way? And look—I'm still standing. When I think about it, not having a boyfriend or the guy of my dreams love me back isn't the worst thing in the world. Does it sting? Yes. Will I get through it? Of course.

"Did you know?" I ask Madelyn.

"Know what?" She replies as she helps herself to the plate of cookies that Mom has kept fully stocked since Parker moved in.

"Know that Brady wasn't into me."

Madelyn sets her cookie down. "It didn't really matter what I thought. You needed to figure that out on your own. Plus, you probably wouldn't have believed me anyway."

She has a point. I've been so blinded by Brady that I've put so many things on hold.

I no longer have any excuses.

Now what?

It's both freeing and scary that I can look beyond Brady. Only in terms of romance. Because I still love him and always will. Just not like *that*.

"We'll always be close friends," I argue. Isn't that what really matters?

Yet, this sinking feeling in my stomach is only partly due to Brady's confession. It's mostly because of Parker.

For perhaps the first time in my life, I wasn't thinking of me when I was consoling Brady. I wasn't hugging him because I wanted him to pick me. I did it because that's what friends do for each other. But Parker probably thinks the worst.

She has every reason to hate me. I don't want her to. Not simply to make me feel better about myself, but because I want to help her.

The door to the garage opens. Parker walks into the kitchen. She pauses when she sees Madelyn and me at the kitchen table.

"Hi," I say, my voice tiny.

"Hi," she replies.

She looks . . . fine. Her cheeks are red and her hair is a little messy, like she's been running. But she doesn't look as big of a mess as I would, given the circumstances.

Let's be serious: If I were faced with an ounce of the crap Parker has dealt with, I wouldn't even be able to get out of bed.

I'm not sure there's anything I can say to make things better, but I'm going to try.

"Oh God, Parker, I'm so—"

She holds her hand up. "Hope, it's fine. Really."

Is it, though?

"I just—"

"Really. Everything is going to be okay."

And the thing is, I believe her. I really do. Who am I to argue with Parker about how things are going to be?

Silence takes over the kitchen.

Then Madelyn pulls out the chair between us and gives Parker a nod. "Hey, Parker."

"Hey, Madelyn."

I haven't told Madelyn everything. She knows enough to know that dirty looks and teasing are no longer allowed. I figure that if Parker wants people to know, she can tell them.

Parker hesitates as she studies the empty chair.

I reach down and grab a cookie, then hold it out to her.

A slight smile spreads on Parker's lips as she walks over, takes the cookie from my hand, and sits down between us.

SIX MONTHS LATER

Hope

I had it all wrong. And I'm big enough to admit it. (Okay, so it took me a while, but I eventually got there and that's all that matters.)

I was focused on the wrong Ps. Sure, I needed Patience, Planning, and Perseverance when it came to building the machines. But what I really needed to focus on was Perspective.

For years, my focus was on getting Brady to be my boyfriend. But what would that have accomplished? Yeah, I would be with Brady, but my life wouldn't magically be perfect. He wouldn't guarantee there wouldn't be struggles.

It's not as if he's out of my life. He's been at college for three weeks and we text almost every day. I'm not going to fool myself into thinking things won't change. He's off making new friends, while I'm focused on the ones I do have. My senior year is all about having fun with Madelyn, getting into a good college, and hopefully winning regionals this year.

"Okay, new crew, listen up!" Conor takes control of the first meeting of our new club. "We have over six months to make the best Rube Goldberg machine possible. This year's challenge is zipping a zipper. We need to make it fun, but also have fun while doing it. There will be times when you'll want to give up and break something, but that's half the battle. But the most important thing to remember is this: Shortcuts make delays."

Wow. That's very poignant of Conor. Maybe this is the year he'll make sense and stop spewing Tolkien.

"But inns make longer ones. At all costs we must keep you away from the *Golden Perch*."

And then he had to keep talking.

"Am I missing something?" Marie, a freshman and new recruit, whispers to me.

"No, that's Conor." I smile at him, happy that he's still part of the team. Fantasy nerdiness and all.

"Okay, but can't we do something better than zip something? What about dropping a needle on a record? That I'd pay to see," says another of our new recruits.

Madelyn.

Yep, my sarcastic best friend has finally broken down and decided to give the club a chance. She said she needed a couple more extracurriculars for her college applications, but I know it's because she was impressed with our machine last year. Not like she'd ever cop to it, but sometimes friends just get each other.

We end the meeting and Madelyn links her arm with mine when we walk out. "Does this make me a nerd now? Although you know that I'd make nerd look hot."

"Of course, total geek chic."

"You need to head home?" she asks.

"Yep, we have dinner with Parker and Hayley tonight."

Mom has insisted that Parker and her sister have dinner with us at least once a week.

While it's nearly impossible to get Madelyn to admit, even begrudgingly, that she likes something (like being in a geeky club), I've tried to be better about not being so stubborn. Or idiotic.

I got used to having Parker around. It was nice having a sister for a while. She was with us for almost three months. It was a little awkward when she and Brady broke up, but the three of us eventually fell into a comfortable pattern. We'd go back and forth to school together. Sometimes Brady would take her to work, sometimes I would. It wasn't because we felt obligated. That's something you have to do because of a job or a family. We did it because we wanted to. Plus, Parker's not that bad.

Okay, okay, okay. I can admit it: I like Parker.

I know, *I know.*

See what I was saying about Perspective. It changes everything.

Parker

I'm not going to lie. It was really rough for a couple of weeks. While I was used to being in seemingly impossible situations, I decided to stop fighting things I couldn't control and returned to Hope's house. It was uncomfortable at first, but then I focused on what I could control, which was studying, saving money, and getting ready for Hayley to return to our home.

I used to hate thinking of the trailer as my home, but it was better than having nothing. Believe me, I'm speaking from experience as someone who truly had nothing. I've had to earn everything I do have, but I don't feel resentful. It makes me feel powerful. Strong. In control.

I hear Hayley's car pull up to the trailer. Now that sound brings me joy.

"Hey!" she greets me with a smile.

She was released from rehab after a month. I always

take time every morning to admire the coins she gets for every sober milestone. I also make sure she knows how much I appreciate her.

"How was school?" she asks as she gives me a hug.

"Good. How was work?"

She got her job back at the salon, where she works four days a week. Hope's dad gave her a part-time job at the dealership in the office doing paper and computer work on the weekend. She's saving money. She's been talking to the guidance counselor at school about finishing her last few classes at college when I leave next year. She's talking about the future.

The future. For so long, Haley and I had been trying to run away from our past. We let our past define us, although in many ways it was hard for it not to. Now we are both truly looking ahead—to things we can control. While nobody knows what the future will bring, there's always a chance something amazing can happen.

I'm not delusional. Things aren't perfect, far from it. We have a long way to go. But at least we're heading in the right direction.

After Hayley and I finish our daily catching up, she heads to her bedroom to change for dinner over at the Kaplans'.

My phone beeps. It's a message from Brady. *Have fun tonight. Eat all of Gabriela's food for me.*

I smile. Who knew breaking up would be the best thing for us? Now when I hear from him or he does something for me, it's because he wants to. Not because he feels sorry for me. Same with Hope. We might actually be considered friends.

And honestly, as painful as it was to have my parents up and leave, it ended the biggest lie in my life: that we were a family.

What I had wasn't a family. My mom wasn't a mom. My dad wasn't a dad. It wasn't real. In a way, they were the ones who did things out of obligation. They fed me, they clothed me, because that's what parents are supposed to do.

None of it was out of love.

Now every relationship I have is because the person wants to be in my life. Hayley's here because she wants to be with me. We're in this together. We'll get through it.

Somehow we will. But it will take time. Bit by bit. Cent by cent. Day by day.

Things are going to be okay.

Author's Note

The idea for this novel came to me way back in 2012, when I had the good fortune to tour with fellow authors Jackson Pearce and Jen Calonita. During our events, Jackson talked about her modern retelling of *The Little Mermaid, Fathomless.* She mentioned that in the Hans Christian Andersen version, the princess who was set to marry the prince wasn't this wicked creature portrayed in the Disney version. She was *just another girl.*

That led me to think about all the contemporary love triangles in books, TV shows, and movies. Often the girlfriend is portrayed as a mean girl. It made it easy for the reader or viewer to know who to cheer for. But what if it wasn't that simple?

When I began developing the two girls at the heart of this story, I wanted to play with the perception people have of each other. You truly don't know somebody until you've spent a day in his or her shoes. Even when I was in high school, I thought I knew my fellow classmates. I lived in a small town. My parents were involved in the community. My mom was even my high school librarian. Years later I discovered that one of my friends' home life was extremely fragile. Another lived in a trailer park. I had no idea. None.

In the age of social media, we all have private and public lives. People are more savvy about the images and perception they put out there. I'm certainly guilty of it. I'm not going to post pictures of me sobbing in my office when I've had a bad day (although maybe I should—being an author is awesome, but it can also be difficult, like any job). Nobody's life is perfect. It's easy to think you know someone if you follow them, but it's a filtered version of his or her life.

Now whenever someone says something rude or acts in a selfish way, I try to give him or her the benefit of the doubt. Maybe the person is having a bad day. Maybe someone he or she loves is sick. Sure, there are still horrible people in the world, but if we act with a lot more compassion with each other, we can all get through this crazy thing we call life. After all, we are all just another girl (or guy) to others.

Acknowledgments

When you've been thinking about/working on a book for five years, you've got a lot of people to thank.

First, to my amazing agent Erin Malone for being Hope and Parker's biggest champion and answering my SOS emails. I'm sorry that this story has made you reevaluate how you treated people in high school—my bad! Special thanks to Sabrina Giglio and everybody at WME for their support.

While my editor, David Levithan, refused to do a *Hamilton*-style rap battle when we had different ideas, he did push me to dig deeper and go *there*. The book is stronger because of him, even if I may require therapy. (I'll be sending you the bills.)

Elizabeth Parisi has, once again, gone above and beyond with my cover. Thank you for taking my tiny idea and turning it into something even better.

Scholastic has been my home through seven (say WHA?) novels, and I'm especially grateful to Erin Black, Sheila Marie Everett, Kelly Ashton, Tracy van Straaten, Lauren Festa, Lizette Serrano, Emily Heddleson, Antonio Gonzalez, Alan Smagler, Leslie Garych, Rebekah Wallin, Liz Byer,

Sue Flynn, Roz Hilden, Nikki Mutch, Terribeth Smith, and all Scholastic sales reps.

I've had to call in friends with special expertise while working on this book. Mary Cele Boockmeier answered all my questions (and did some story brainstorming) about social services and Parker's family life. Andrew Harwell helped me with the D&D references and has a very high charisma score in his own right. I called on Cecilia Barragán and Dania Mejia at Penguin Random House Mexico to add some flavor to Hope's mom. Dawne Frickson Pafford wasn't alarmed when I asked her about money laundering (which is more a reflection on my character than hers!). And, of course, Kirk Benshoff for keeping my website running smoothly.

I'm so fortunate to be part of a wonderful community of YA authors. For years, I would talk about this book with friends who offered their support, especially when I knew I was making things worse for Parker (and therefore myself). Big, sloppy kisses to Jennifer Lynn Barnes, Sarah Rees Brennan, Rose Brock, Ally Carter, Carrie Ryan, Kieran Scott, and Jennifer E. Smith.

Writing about Parker made me appreciate how lucky I am to have the family that I have. As much as I probably gave my parents and siblings reasons to want to abandon me as a teen, they stuck with me.

Finally, huge thanks to the booksellers, librarians, bloggers, and readers who have shared my books with others. The best gift you could ever give an author is to tell another person about a book you love. This career is a gift, one that I will never take for granted.